SNOOPING CAN BE

Helpful—Sometimes

SNOOPING CAN BE

Helpful—Sometimes

LINDA HUDSON HOAGLAND

Jan-Carol
Publishing, Inc
"every story needs a book"

SNOOPING CAN BE HELPFUL—SOMETIMES

LINDA HUDSON HOAGLAND

Published May 2016
Little Creek Books
Imprint of Jan-Carol Publishing, Inc
All rights reserved
Copyright © 2016

ISBN: 978-1-939289-94-0
Library of Congress Control Number: 2016942419

You may contact the publisher:
Jan-Carol Publishing, Inc
PO Box 701
Johnson City, TN 37605
publisher@jancarolpublishing.com
jancarolpublishing.com

This book is dedicated to my family:
Mike, Sherry, Matt and Becky

DEAR READER

Lindsay Harris tries to help her fourteen year old daughter, Emily, locate her missing friend, Maddie, who is a homeless teenager.

If you have any feelings at all, you have probably run into a similar situation in your lifetime. I know I have.

Lindsay opens her heart and welcomes a complete stranger into her family that includes herself and three children of her own.

Having been a legal secretary/assistant in my earlier years, I knew Lindsay's task wasn't going to be easy but it was doable.

There are other forces out in the world that want to prevent that little family inclusion from taking place. Lindsay, her best friends, Jed and Marnie, along with her children, Emily, Ellen, and Ryan, all band together to fight those forces as best they can.

This is the fifth volume of *A Lindsay Harris Murder Mystery Series* and it deals with some of the realities of the world of the homeless.

As Lindsay delves into that world, she discovers that *SNOOP-ING CAN BE HELPFUL– SOMETIMES.*

Yours truly,
Linda Hudson Hoagland

Acknowledgments

Janie C. Jessee, publisher of eight of my books, must be acknowledged for allowing me to do what I most like to do: write.

A special thanks to Tammy Robinson Smith for asking me to start this little series.

Chapter 1

"Mom, Maddie is missing," said Emily, as she walked through the kitchen doorway after climbing down from the school bus.

"Didn't you tell me she was homeless?" I asked. I placed a few snacks out for them to grab from the counter on their way to their rooms.

"Yes...yes, but she came to school every day, until this week. She hasn't been there at all for the last five days," said Emily with concern evident in her voice.

"Maybe she's moved on," I said, trying to console my worried daughter.

"No, she said she would let me know if that happened. I think something has happened to her," said Emily.

"Maybe not; like I said, she has probably pulled up stakes and found another place to live," I said.

"No, she would have told me," said Emily. Her anger was beginning to show.

"Is she still living at the address she gave the school?" I asked.

"No, she lives in the empty house on Vine Street," said Emily.

"You mean the old Harold house? That place is close to falling down!" I said in astonishment.

"She doesn't have a choice, if she wants to go to school," said Emily sullenly.

"What do you expect me to do? I'm not her mother. I'm not even a distant relative," I said in exasperation.

"She needs help, Mom. Why can't we help her?" pleaded Emily.

"I guess we can do something, Em. I just don't know where to start," I said.

"Let's go to the house on Vine Street," suggested Emily.

"Okay, we'll do that tomorrow. We're going to the movie theater this evening. Remember?" I said.

"Oh, yeah, I forgot," said Emily. She ran through the kitchen so she could dump her school books on the bed in her room.

Ellen, Emily's twin sister, poked her head into the kitchen and asked, "What do we have to eat?"

"It's on the counter. We'll get pizza later, after the movie," I said.

"What are we celebrating?" asked Ellen.

"Life," I answered with a smile.

"What's that supposed to mean?" asked Ryan as he popped out from behind his sister.

"It means that I'm grateful to have a job, a home, and a wonderful family," I answered.

"Aw, Mom, there's got to be another reason. We don't all go out unless something has happened. Now, what's up?" he prodded me.

"Nothing, really. I just want to take my kids to the movies and eat pizza. Isn't that reason enough?" I asked.

"Yes, Mom," Ryan said sarcastically

"Eat your snack and get ready to go, okay?" I said, trying to get him moving and away from the desire to aggravate me.

Unfortunately, Ryan was right. We didn't usually get to go to the movies and then out to eat. Money was in short supply, and I found it difficult to pay the bills sometimes.

The extra money I was going to splurge with came from an income tax refund. I was determined my kids were going to have a little bit of fun.

I let them pick the movie, once we all got into the car. When they all came to agreement, I started the engine.

When we entered the theater Emily sat next to me, while Ryan and Ellen scattered out to sit with friends.

"Why aren't you sitting with your friends, Em?" I asked my quiet, pensive daughter.

"I'd rather sit beside you," she answered in a whisper.

"Why?" I asked.

"You're my mom, that's why. Don't you want me to sit here?" she asked in a loud whisper.

"Of course I do. I just thought you would rather be with one of your friends," I suggested.

"My friend is gone," she said softly.

Chapter 2

I had hoped the trip home from the pizza place would be short and sweet. The kids were tired, as was I—until Emily shrieked and pointed to a person walking along the side of the road.

"What is it?" I asked as I tried to calm my nerves. That shriek had caught me totally unprepared.

"That's Maddie! It looks like Maddie," she said loudly. She pointed to the figure that had started to run into the shadows.

"Are you sure?" I asked, slowing the car to pull over to the side of the road.

"No—but it sure did look like her," she said excitedly.

"Did you see where she ran off to?" I asked. I looked out the windows to see if I could find her.

"No, she took off into the darkness, over there by those trees. We'll never find her in the dark. Can we look for her tomorrow, Mom?" pleaded Emily.

"Yes, Honey, we'll try to find her," I said, as I tried to figure out how I was going to fit that in with everything else I had to do.

As I pulled back onto the road, I gave the darkness of the trees another quick glance. I saw nothing but the dark, hulking trees.

"Emily, watch the side of the road. That might not have been Maddie. She might be up ahead, or we'll find her tomorrow. Okay?" I asked Emily. She stared wide-eyed out of the passenger side window

"Everybody out!" I shouted when I pulled onto the driveway. Ryan and Ellen had dozed off, but Emily continued to stare out of the window.

The two sleepyheads shuffled into the house to their respective rooms as Emily swung her head from side to side, trying to capture our entire little world in her sight line.

"Emily, get in the house and go to bed. I promise you we will look for Maddie tomorrow," I whispered as I gave her a little shove.

Bedtime preparations didn't take long for any of us. I had a feeling in the pit of my stomach that blissful sleep wasn't in the cards for me.

My head hit the pillow and I was gone, until a tap on my door startled me into wakefulness.

"What? Who is it?" I stammered.

"It's me, Emily," said a low voice through the door. I could tell she was trying not to awaken her brother and sister.

"Come in, Em," I said, when I figured out how to answer her. The fog of sleep was clouding my mind.

My bedroom door opened slowly and Emily slipped inside, closing the door behind her.

"What's wrong?" I asked although I already knew the answer to that question.

"I can't sleep, Mom. I'm worried about Maddie," she said as her eyes started to tear up

"I know, Baby. But there's nothing we can do about it tonight. You need to go on to bed, or we'll be too tired to look for her," I said soothingly.

5

Emily was my serious child. She was the second half of a set of identical twins, but the emotions were not split to reflect their sameness

Ellen seemed to have received the carefree, happy gene. Emily received the worry gene. Otherwise, they were identical twins.

"Can I sleep with you, Mom?" she asked with a whimper.

"Don't you think you're a little too old for that?" I asked with a smile, as I pulled the covers back to let her crawl in.

"Never," she said, snuggling up to me.

Chapter 3

At six o'clock my eyes popped open as if something had awakened me with a jarring sound. I don't think I heard a sound; I just felt it.

Emily had curled up and was sleeping peacefully, so I wanted to crawl out of the bed without disturbing her.

I needed to take a look around to find out what had pulled me from sleep, if indeed anything or anyone did.

I inched my way carefully and slowly off the bed, grabbed my robe, and left my bedroom, walking to the living room so I could look out the front window.

I didn't see anything that looked out of place. There were no strange cars parked on the street. No strangers were milling around, and no stray animals were wandering around unleashed.

"Oh well," I mumbled, as I entered the kitchen to make the coffee that I so desperately needed.

After I started the coffee brewing, I decided to button my robe and slip outside to get my newspaper that had been placed in the box directly across the street from my house.

I pushed against the storm door to let myself out onto the porch, and found it stuck. Something was preventing me from opening the door. I pulled the door almost closed, but still open wide enough to get my hand through the gap to the outside; I felt around blindly, hunting for what was causing the blockage.

I got a whiff of something that smelled bad: *really* bad.

I continued to feel around, looking for whatever was preventing me from opening the door, but I was almost afraid of what I was going to find. Judging by the foul odor that was assaulting my nose, it was nothing good.

I kept pushing on the door and I felt it give a little. I pushed harder, and it moved enough for me to squeeze through the opening to get outside and find out what was on my front porch.

"Oh my *God!*" I screamed as I stared at the grotesque body of a dead cat.

The cat had a rope tied around its neck, and it was black in color.

"This is the wrong time of the year for killing black cats," I mumbled as I re-entered the house in search of a garbage bag.

Ryan came to the living room in search of me.

"Don't go outside right now," I told him as I walked past him into the kitchen.

"Why?" asked Ryan.

"There's a dead cat on the front porch. Someone must have thrown him onto the porch, because that cat couldn't have crawled up there," I explained.

"Who would do that?" asked Ryan.

"I don't know," I whispered. I walked past him again with garbage bag in hand. I opened the garbage bag so I could cover the carcass with it and then pick it up, allowing the cat's body to fall to the bottom of the bag.

"Mom, why would anyone do that?" asked Ellen. She poked her head out the door as I was trying to pick up the mess.

"I don't know, Honey," I answered, with a grimace from the smell. "Do you have any enemies? Maybe Emily has an enemy."

"I don't know anyone who would do something like that. I don't know about Emily. She has some pretty strange friends," said Ellen.

"Are you talking about Maddie?" I asked.

"No, she's the one who is almost normal, if you know what I mean," Ellen whispered

"What about Emily's other friends? Why are the strange?" I asked with interest.

"You have to see them, Mom. They are always dressed in black. They have tattoos and rings in odd places. They wear white base makeup, black lipstick, and all the girls plus some of the boys have long, stringy, black hair. They are the darkest gothic-looking bunch I have ever seen," said Ellen, with a shiver traveling through her small body.

"Emily doesn't dress like that. Why would she want friends who look like that?" I asked.

"You got me, Mom. I don't know," answered Ellen. She wrinkled her nose and walked into the kitchen to get away from the putrid smell.

"Ellen, unlock the back door for me. I don't want to carry this garbage bag through the house," I shouted.

"Okay," Ellen shouted in response.

I walked on the sidewalk and pavement as far as I could go, but eventually I had to step off into the wet, dew-covered grass. I dropped the cat's body into an empty garbage can, with the thought that I might have to call the town police and report the incident.

I was still in my nightgown and robe, so I hurried to the back door to get off the wet grass. When I reached the wooden steps that led to the small porch, I was shocked to see that they were covered with a dark red, sticky substance.

"That's blood!" I screamed. "Ellen, did you see this? Who in the world is doing this to my house?"

The response I got from Ellen was "Yuck."

I did not enter the house through the back door. I didn't want to track through the blood. I walked to the front and ran into the house, yelling at my children.

"Everybody up and out of bed!" I shouted loudly.

I wanted them up and ready to help me clean the mess up after I called the police.

Chapter 4

"Stillwell Town Police, may I help you?" asked a professional voice.

"I need to report some vandalism. My name is Lindsay Harris," I said politely, then waited for the transfer to go through.

"Ms. Harris, what kind of vandalism are you wanting to report?" asked an uninterested, masculine voice.

"Someone threw or placed a dead black cat on my front porch, and covered my back porch steps in blood," I answered trying to stir his interest.

"Did you say blood, ma'am?" asked the voice. It had perked up with obvious interest.

"Yes, I did. Could you send an officer to my house to take a look, please?" I said. I gave him my address and phone number before I disconnected the call.

I wanted to clean up both messes, but I had to wait so the officer could see them. There was blood, and other body fluids, on the front porch where the cat had been placed. I would take the officer around to the back of the house to the garbage can to see the actual remains.

In the meantime, I needed to talk with Emily. She was the only one of my children I had not questioned.

"Em, do you know anyone who would throw a dead cat onto the front porch and pour blood on the back steps?" I asked, as my unsuspecting daughter entered the kitchen.

"What? Dead cat? Blood? What are you talking about?" Emily sputtered. She shook her head in denial.

"Do you know anyone who owns a black cat?" I asked softly.

"Maddie has one that stays with her. It didn't have a home either, so they became attached. She takes him with her when she moves to another sleeping place," said Emily.

"Have you seen the black cat?" I asked.

"Yes," she answered timidly

"After you get dressed and eat breakfast, I will show you the cat. You can tell me if it belongs to Maddie, okay?" I asked softly, so as not to get Emily all bent out of shape with an accusation.

Emily nodded and turned to leave the kitchen. She raced up the steps and was back in no time at all, fully dressed.

"We are going to look for Maddie, aren't we, Mom?" she pleaded.

"Yes, Em, just as soon as the police get here, look at the mess, and leave. I need to tell them about this mess, just in case it happens again."

"Why, Mom?" asked Emily.

"Why what?"

"Why would anyone do that?" asked Emily.

"Do you know anyone who might be upset with you? Would any of your new friends do this?" I asked sternly.

"Ellen has been talking to you, hasn't she?" demanded Emily.

"All Ellen said was that you had some strange friends," I said defensively.

"No, my friends wouldn't do this," Emily said angrily. "What about Ellen's friends? They are just a bunch of snooty, stuck-up snobs."

"What happened to the two of you?" I said with concern. "You used to like the same people."

"I just found out how shallow and mindless those people were. I wanted to make my own friends, people I could trust," answered Emily.

A knock on the front door ended my conversation with Emily.

Chapter 5

"I'm Officer Johnson," said the tall young man on my porch. He was dressed in the dark brown uniform of the Stillwell Police Department.

"I'm Lindsay Harris, and we can start right here on the front porch," I said. I pointed to the putrid smelling blood and body fluids puddled on the wooden floor. "I had already carried the black cat to the back and placed it in the garbage can before I discovered what had happened in the back. I'll show you the cat's remains when we finish here."

Officer Johnson started writing some information onto the sheet of paper he had attached to a clipboard.

"The biggest mess is in the back," I said, leading him around the house to see the back steps.

"That *is* a mess," said Officer Johnson.

The next show and tell item was in the garbage can. I motioned for Emily to come over with me, because I wanted her to see the cat.

I pulled the bag from the plastic can, opened the top, and exposed the grotesque remains of the poor cat for all to see

"Someone strangled that cat," said Officer Johnson before turning his head away from the ugly sight.

"That's Maddie's cat," whispered Emily

"I was afraid of that," I whispered. I pulled Emily in close so she could lay her head against my shoulder.

"Why would anyone do that to Maddie's cat?" asked Emily, through the falling tears that were streaking down her cheeks.

"I don't know, Baby, but we will try to find out," I said, as I tried to console her.

"Ma'am, do you have any enemies?" asked Officer Johnson.

"None that I am aware of, sir. I checked with my kids, and they don't have any idea who would do this," I answered.

"Who is Maddie? Does she own the cat?" asked Officer Johnson.

Emily was still crying, so I answered for her. "Maddie is Emily's friend from school, and she has a black cat that looks like this one."

"I will file this report and keep my eyes open for any more incidents like this one. In the meantime, keep your eyes and ears open for any further damage. Give us a call if you need any help," said the officer. He then walked to his vehicle, which was parked in front of my house.

I knew there was nothing they would or could do, because of the lack of witnesses and the fact that we had no known enemies. All I wanted to do was to get it on the record.

As soon as the policeman left, I ran into the house to get a bucket of soapy water to wash away the blood and body fluids before they had a chance to get bone dry. Then I moved to the back steps to wash off all of the blood. I didn't even know if it was human blood or animal blood, and that worried me.

With the cleaning tasks completed, I asked Ellen, Emily, and Ryan to get into the car. We were going to find Maddie.

15

Chapter 6

I knew Emily wanted to search for her friend, but I thought maybe Ryan and Ellen might balk at the suggestion.

I was so wrong.

Ryan and Ellen wanted to find some excitement while Emily was looking for her missing friend.

"Where is Maddie Stevens living now?" I asked Emily as I climbed into the car. Emily was sitting in the front seat beside me.

"I told you, she was living on Vine Street. You called it the Harold house," said Emily.

"To Vine Street we will go. When we get there, we all need to stay together for safety reasons. We really don't know what we will be running into," I said with caution.

"Mom, quit trying to scare us," said Ryan,

"It's the truth, Ryan. Now, promise to do as I say," I told my impetuous son.

"Okay, okay," Ryan said with a grin.

The Harold house was actually within walking distance, but I thought it was better to go in the car, again, for safety reasons. I was determined to keep us all together, and of course, to keep us all safe from any kind of harm.

I parked the car directly in front of the Harold house.

"Now, we all need to stay close to each other," I said again when we crawled from the car. "Watch your step, because this house has been empty for a long time. Anything, man or animal, could be hiding in here."

We must have been a sight to see. All four of us were crouched over sneaking up to the Harold house in plain sight, walking on the cracked, broken sidewalk.

The front door had a board nailed across it, but when I reached for the doorknob it turned easily. I pushed the door and it banged against the wall on the inside of the house. The open space beneath the board was wide enough for me to crawl through and stand inside. I was followed by Emily, Ryan, and Ellen.

Inside the Harold house, we all stood and looked around to get our bearings.

"Maddie, are you in here?" shouted Emily.

There was no answer, so I took a few steps forward to look into a different area.

The living room where we had entered looked relatively clean compared to the room to the right. It was filled with trash and debris consisting of old clothes, automobile parts, appliance parts, and whatever else the scavenger who assembled the pile of junk could pick up and carry.

Obviously Maddie was not hiding in that mess, so I traveled on to the next room.

Again, it was filled with junk lining the walls, except this time, the pieces of junk were larger items. It looked as if someone had been preparing for a huge yard sale.

I continued on to the next room with the kids in tow; it proved to be the kitchen, or what was left of a kitchen. The sink had been ripped off the wall, the cabinets had been pulled down, and an old electric range was still upright but missing the electric burners, the oven door, and the storage drawers.

There was a small room off of the kitchen that was probably the laundry room, and next to it was what was left of a bathroom: broken tub, missing sink, and falling plaster.

"Did you guys see the steps that go upstairs?" I asked, shaking my head at all of this mess.

"Yeah, it's on the left side of the front door, in a hallway there," said Ryan.

"Let's backtrack and check out the upstairs," I said, as I turned to leave the kitchen area.

There was absolutely no sign of Maddie living on the first floor, so I had hopes of finding something on the second floor.

We waded back through the trash and debris to reach the living room, which led to the room that held the staircase.

Chapter 7

"Where's Emily?" I asked. I looked around the small room where the staircase was located.

"She went on ahead," said Ryan with a shrug of his shoulders.

"I told you guys to stay together," I mumbled, as I started to climb the stairs. "Please be careful. There is a lot of loose trash on these steps."

I glanced around and saw Ryan and Ellen gingerly stepping up behind me.

"Maddie, are you here?" said Emily from a room to the right of the little hallway at the top of the stairs.

"Emily, stay right where you are. We will come to you," I said loudly.

"Mom, there's blood in here. It looks pretty fresh," said Emily, with fear etching her voice.

We entered the room where Emily was kneeling on the floor, looking at a puddle of blood and a paper that was showing through the red glaze.

"Look at this, Mom. It's a note to me, and it's signed by Maddie. She knew I would come looking for her," said Emily, with more excitement than I had seen in her for a couple of days.

"What does the note say, Em?" I asked. I tried to equal her excitement.

Emily,
He found me. He will kill me if I don't go with him. We can't go far because he doesn't have a car. Get help and please find me.
Maddie

"Who took her, Emily?" I asked.

"Her father took her. He does some really bad things with her, and she wasn't supposed to tell anybody. She told me, and now he will kill her so she can't tell anyone else. That's why she ran away from home, to get away from him," said Emily, fighting tears again,

"Well, I think our next step in this adventure is to drive around and look for unoccupied houses," I said. I turned to go back down the stairs.

When we were walking to the car, Emily asked, "Mom, why would Maddie's father treat her so badly?"

"Some people are just plain sick in the head, and they can never be healed," I answered with a frown.

"Dad would never do anything like that, would he?" asked Emily.

"No, Em. Your father would never ever do anything like that to any of you. He and I may not be married anymore, but I know he would never hurt you," I said with a smile.

"What kind of bad things?" asked Ryan.

Emily looked at me, but said nothing. It was up to me to tell him.

"Ryan, he was doing to Maddie something that only moms and dads should do," I said, not wanting to get into graphic detail.

"Oh," he said. He let the subject drop as did I.

After we all climbed back into the car, we were all quiet for short time. I guessed the idea of living a life like Maddie had given them food for thought.

Chapter 8

"Emily, I don't know where we should go. Do you have any ideas?" I asked, starting the car.

"Can we just drive around for a while? Then maybe we should tell the police," Emily suggested

"Sounds good to me," I said, as I continued on my way.

"There's an empty house on the next street," said Ryan. "My school bus goes past it every day. I've never seen anyone there, and the lights are never on."

I made a right turn, and drove slowly so I could see everything that might be happening on the street.

"How far up, Ryan?" I asked.

"Just a little further," he answered.

I think I spotted the empty house before he did. As I slowed down to take a better look, he started jumping around and pointing from the back seat.

"That's it! Over there, Mom," he shouted.

"Okay, Ryan, calm down," I said. I pulled the car to the curb.

There was a *For Sale* sign leaning over in the front yard nestled in the tall grass.

We all gathered on the front porch to look in the windows and check to see if we could open the front door.

"It's locked, guys," I said. "Let's walk around to the back."

I glanced around to see if the neighbors on both sides were home; they were. My hope was that they wouldn't call the police on us.

They didn't. One of them called the real estate agent whose name was listed on the sign.

He pulled his vehicle onto the driveway with a flurry of gravel.

We were just starting to walk around the back of the house.

"Can I show you the inside?" asked the agent, a man dressed in a gray business suit.

"You guys be quiet," I said. "We'll let him show us the house."

"Yes, sure. We were walking around back to see how much land was included," I said, winging it.

We pretended to take in the small back yard, then we walked to the front of the house where the man, whose name was Bud Simpson, let us in to look around.

The house was an older model requiring a lot of remodeling, which would definitely lower the market value.

We all traipsed through the entire house, looking inside closets and searching for signs of occupancy. When we found nothing, I thanked Bud Simpson and went on my way. By that time, Ellen and Ryan were ready to go home.

"Emily, we're going to have to stop looking for now. I've got laundry to do, among other things."

"But, Mom, the note said she needed help," Emily said

"We'll call the police as soon as we get home and tell them where to find the note and the blood. Then they can start hunting for her," I said, to calm Emily's pleas.

"Do you think they will?" Emily asked.

"Yes, especially after they see the note," I answered.

"I hope so," said Emily in a whisper.

Chapter 9

My cell phone started buzzing as soon as I turned onto my driveway.

"Hello?" I answered.

"Linds, this is Jed. What's up?"

"The kids and I have been out looking for Emily's missing friend," I answered, as if it were an everyday occurrence.

"You're kidding," he said in a surprised tone.

"I wish I were."

"Do you need some help?" Jed asked.

"All I can get. I have a very unhappy daughter, because her friend is missing," I said.

"Which one? Which daughter?" he asked.

"Emily, the one who forever will be so serious about everything."

"What happened to her friend," Jed asked.

I started explaining the whole tale to Jed as I walked inside the house. The kids headed for the kitchen in search of snacks.

It was so good to talk with someone who was interested in what I had to say, and wasn't my offspring.

"Are you going to go out looking again tomorrow?" asked Jed.

"Probably."

"What time?" he asked.

"Sometime after church. Do you want to come with us?" I asked.

"Yeah, that might make a good human interest story," he said,

Jed was a features writer for the biggest newspaper in the area. On occasion, he would give me a call to get ideas for a future article. That's probably what he was doing when he called this time too, but that was okay. I could use the help.

As soon as I disconnected from Jed's call, I called the local non-emergency police line. I needed to do some explaining to them, and I didn't want to tie up the 9-1-1 line.

I managed to get Officer Johnson again, the same officer who came to the house for the vandalism call.

"Officer Johnson, this is Lindsay Harris again, and I have a peculiar story to tell you that might take a little time. Is that all right with you?"

"Yes ma'am, what is the problem?" he asked politely.

I started the spiel again, the same one I had related to Jed.

"This homeless girl, how do you know she just hasn't moved on?" he asked.

"The note showing through the blood specifically said she needed help," I said impatiently.

"I need the address of that house, ma'am," said the police officer, as he realized that my feathers were being ruffled.

"Will you check it out? Can I call you back and see if there is any progress with locating Maddie? She is my daughter's friend, and she is so worried about Maddie," I said, when he finally seemed interested.

"Yes ma'am, you can call any time; or, if you prefer, I will call you as soon as I check on the house. At that time, I might need more information about the missing girl," said Officer Johnson.

"Great," I said. "I will give you my cell phone number so you can reach me anywhere," I said excitedly.

After reciting my cell phone number to Officer Johnson, I disconnected the call with a feeling of accomplishment. Hopefully the police would think Maddie was important enough to help her. If not, I would find Maddie, with the help of Jed and my kids, and show her that all adults were not like her father. That was important to me.

Another important thought was that I wanted my children to know that I would have their backs. Emily needed me to cover her back.

Chapter 10

Sunday arrived with a ringing telephone.

"Hello," I croaked weakly. I wasn't awake enough for a conversation yet.

"Linds."

"Jed, what time is it?" I asked.

"Seven," he replied sheepishly.

"Oh," I said softly.

"Were you sleeping?" he asked.

"No, I was awake. I just hadn't crawled out of bed yet," I explained.

"I'm so sorry. I guess I should have waited. I didn't even think about the early hour. Now that I have you, how is the search for the missing girl going?" he asked excitedly.

"The police are investigating, but they weren't very interested at the beginning," I answered.

"Do you think your friend Marnie could find any records on Maddie and/or her family at the courthouse?" he asked.

"Yeah, I guess she could, when she gets a chance. I'll give her a call today. If I beg really hard, maybe she could find something for me tomorrow," I said.

"Yes, that would be good. Are you going to be home in an hour or so?" Jed asked.

"Yes, I don't think I'll go to church today. I'm going to let the kids sleep a little longer. We were up pretty late, looking for Maddie and talking with the police. They could use the rest. I don't think God will be too mad at us, do you?" I said.

"No, He will understand, and I will be on my way. We can do a little looking together, okay?" Jed said.

As soon as the conversation ended, I jumped into the shower so I could start my day on a good note.

The coffee had just finished brewing when I heard a knock at the door. I jerked it open, thinking Jed would be standing here.

It wasn't Jed.

"Officer Johnson, what do you need?" I asked after closing my mouth, which had opened in total surprise.

"As I told you before, I will need some information about the missing girl," he said softly.

"My daughter, Emily, will have to tell you about her. I've never actually met her. Come inside, and I will go wake her," I said hurriedly as I left the living room. "Please have a seat. I won't be but a minute."

I ran down the hallway knocking on all the doors, but stopping at Emily's.

"Emily, get up now. Officer Johnson need to talk with you," I said loudly.

When I didn't get a response, I pushed open the door.

Her bed was empty.

The bathroom door was standing open, so I could see she wasn't in there.

"Oh no, not again," I mumbled.

I wiped the look of panic from my face, walked to Ellen's door, and knocked. When Ellen opened the door I said, "Where is your sister?"

"In her room, I guess," said Ellen. She glanced away from my gaze, which was a telltale sign that she wasn't being truthful.

"Ellen, I need the truth," I said sternly.

"She went looking for Maddie," mumbled Ellen.

"Where?" I demanded.

"She went back to that house," stammered Ellen.

"The one where the blood is? Did she go there?" I asked sternly.

"I think so. She said she was really worried about Maddie. Please don't be mad at her, Mom," said Ellen.

"Okay, all right, first things first. I need you to get dressed and go downstairs to talk with Officer Johnson. You need to tell him everything you know about Maddie Stevens. You need to be Emily for Officer Johnson, do you understand?" When Ellen nodded her head in agreement, I continued, "When you tell him what you know, we will go hunt for Emily," I said hurriedly.

I left Ellen's room and heard someone knocking on the door. When I opened it, Jed was standing there with a big grin on his face and a big box of doughnuts in his hands.

"Breakfast! Great! Come in, Jed," I said with a smile, hiding my frustration over Emily's departure.

As soon as Jed saw Officer Johnson, he stopped dead in his tracks.

"Jed, this is Officer Johnson. He is investigating Maddie's disappearance. Emily is getting dressed so she can tell him all she knows about Maddie," I explained hurriedly.

"You are?" asked the officer as he extended his hand and directed the question to Jed.

"Jed Thompson, friend of the family."

Ellen entered the room and stopped directly in front of Officer Johnson.

"Mom said I have to tell you everything I know about Madelyn Stevens," said Ellen in a very business-like tone.

"Yes, young lady, what can you tell me?" asked Officer Johnson as he almost smiled.

"My sister, Em— err, Ellen, might know more about her than I do but she isn't home right now. I'll tell you what I know."

Officer Johnson held a pad of paper and pen at ready to write down everything that was pertinent.

"Maddie Stevens is my age, 14, and she's a new girl in the school. She has long brown hair, and dresses a little funny sometimes," said Ellen, trying very hard to be Emily.

"What do you mean by dressing funny?" asked the officer.

"Well, she wears long skirts a lot, and long sleeves even in the hottest weather. She has really pale skin and freckles. She would really be a cute girl if she would dress better, more like everyone else, but after what she told me about her family and being abused, I guess she can't because she doesn't have the money to buy any," added Ellen sadly.

"How tall is she?" asked of officer.

"She is about the same height that I am, so I guess about 5'2" and she is thin, really, really thin," Ellen said as she paused for a moment. "I guess she didn't have very much to eat if she was homeless."

"Why was she homeless?" asked the officer.

"She told me she was abused. Maddie's mom is dead, and her daddy made her do everything for him her mom couldn't do. That's against the law, isn't it?" asked Ellen.

"Yes, it is especially if sex was involved," said the officer.

"Maddie said he did bad things to her almost weekly. That would be so awful," said Ellen, trying to remain in her role as Emily.

"Have you seen her father? Do you know what he looks like?" asked Officer Johnson.

"No sir, I haven't seen him. That's why she keeps moving from place to place," answered Ellen.

"I think this is about all I need from you, for now," he said, looking up from his notepad at Ellen.

"Officer Johnson, what did you find out at the Harold house? Was the note still there? Did you see the blood?" I asked.

"Mrs. Harris, the note was gone and the blood had been cleaned up. They didn't do a very good job of cleaning, though, so it was easy to find," he answered.

"You are going to look for Maddie, aren't you?" I asked.

"Yes ma'am."

The officer left and the rest of us grabbed doughnuts and ran to the car. We needed to find Emily, again.

Chapter 11

"Where did Ellen go? You did mean Ellen, since Emily is right here, right?" said a confused Jed.

"No, this is Ellen. She was pretending to be Emily for the officer. I didn't want him to know that Emily has sneaked out of the house to look for Maddie. At least, I didn't want him to know until I went to find her," I explained.

"Where did Emily go?" asked Jed.

"I think she went back to the Harold house. That's about a mile from our house. She must have started walking as soon as it started to get light outside," I said.

"Why didn't she wait for all of us to go?" asked Jed.

"Honestly, I don't know. She was just so worried about Maddie, I guess," I answered. "She really needs to stop taking off on her own. I'm going to have to talk to her when we find her again."

"It's that house, isn't it, Mom?" asked Ellen, as she pointed to the Harold house.

"Yes, I'll park in front. I think it would be safer to do that," I said. I aimed the car to the side of the road. "You all need to just sit tight and look out the windows to see if there is any noticeable movement coming from inside."

"Aww, Mom," said Ryan

"Just sit, Ryan. We don't know what or who is inside," I said sternly.

"Maybe we should go in first and then tell the kids to come in," I whispered to Jed.

"That sounds like a good idea," he agreed.

When I entered the Harold house the night before, I'd walked inside without much thought for my own safety. This time, I was wary of trouble jumping out and grabbing me.

Jed was with me, but that didn't matter; something or someone could grab him, too.

"Jed, this might be dangerous," I whispered.

"Yeah, I know," he said softly.

"Did you bring anything for defense?" I asked.

He held up his fists and said, "Just these."

"That will have to do," I said with a weak smile.

We walked onto the porch and stopped to look and listen. We tried to peek into the front window, but it was covered with what looked like an old, dirty bed sheet.

I couldn't hear a sound other than my own breathing and the noisy birds, flying and chattering loudly.

"We might as well go on inside. I can't see or hear anything out here," said Jed. "Stand behind me, Linds, when I open the door."

I could feel myself start to bristle a bit. I had been on my own too long for anyone to think he could just take over.

"Macho man, are you?" I said with a forced laugh.

"Just do it," said Jed.

"Okay, let's go," I said. I tugged on his shirttail.

Jed twisted the knob and pushed on the door, but it didn't budge.

"Is this the way you went inside yesterday?" he asked with concern.

"Yes," I whispered.

"Let's walk around to the back," he said.

My trouble radar activated when a chill raced up and down my spine.

"Wait a minute, Jed," I whispered.

We stood and listened again. This time I could hear noises; exactly what they were, I didn't have a clue. At about the same time, I caught a glimpse of a figure running away from the house. It was a homeless person. I was sure of that much, but it was a younger man. His limber, scrawny body led me to believe it was not Maddie's father.

"What is that?" asked Jed.

"It's a scratching sound. Let's try the front door again," I said as I reached for the doorknob.

"Wait a minute," shouted Jed.

Too late, I had already started leaning against the door. It opened a little so I leaned harder.

"It's moving," I shouted.

Jed leaned his shoulder against the door and we managed to get it open far enough to wiggle through, only to behold a sight we weren't expecting to see.

"Emily!" I screamed.

She was what was blocking the door. She was on the floor, hands and feet tied up, with duct tape across her mouth. It must have been her making the scratching noises.

Jed pulled out a pocket knife and cut her hands and feet loose from their bindings.

"Do you want me to give the tape a jerk? It will hurt, but I think it will be easier on you if I pull it fast," I told Emily, as she bobbed her head up and down.

I jerked the tape and she screamed. She covered her mouth with her freed hands. Tears streamed down her dirty cheeks.

"Who did this to you?" I asked her, pulling her close to me in a big embrace.

At first Emily didn't speak. All she could do was sob.

I waited.

"Maddie's father tied me up," she said finally.

"Was Maddie with him?" I asked.

"Yes, but she didn't want to be. He found her here and made her leave with him," Emily continued. "There was another man here, but I don't think he wanted any part of this."

"When we get back home, I want you to tell all of this to Officer Johnson," I said sternly.

"I can't, Mom. He will kill Maddie if I do," she said. The tears started flowing again.

"Do you know where he took her?" I asked as I tried to console her.

"No," she said. She continued to cry and shake her head to emphasize her negative answer.

"Come on, Emily. Let's go to the car and go home. You can tell me about everything after you take a shower, put on some clean clothes, and rest for a while. Okay?" I asked.

Chapter 12

"Jed, I'm going to give Marnie a call. I want to see if she can help us get some information about the Stevens family," I said when everything was quiet at home.

"Sounds good. Do you want me to leave to give you some privacy?" Jed asked politely.

"No way, you are part of this. Just stay right there," I said.

I punched in the number and listened while it rang.

"Hello?" said a breathless voice.

"Marnie?" I asked.

"Lindsay, how are you? It's been a while since we talked," Marnie said, in a scolding tone.

"I know, I'm sorry I haven't called sooner, but life tends to get in the way," I said in explanation.

"Yes, I know what you mean. What can I do for you?" asked Marnie.

"I need some information," I said shyly.

"I figured that out. What is it?" asked a sarcastic Marnie.

"I need to know something about a family named Stevens," I said.

"Are they from around here?" asked Marnie.

"They are now, but I don't know if they are from here originally," I explained.

"Stevens is the last name. I need a first name," said Marnie.

"The only one I have right now is for the fourteen-year-old daughter. She is the reason we need the information. She is a friend of Emily's, and she is homeless," I continued.

"Oh. That may be a problem, since she's a juvenile, but I'll see what I can do tomorrow. Do you want me to call you at work?" Marnie asked.

"Yes, please. Emily is very worried about Maddie. Maddie's father actually tied Emily up and left her lying on the dirty floor at the empty Harold house. She knows he's dangerous," I explained further.

""Is Emily okay? Did you call the police?" asked Marnie.

"Yes, and no. Emily is okay, but a bit shaken, and no, we didn't call the police. Emily said Maddie's father threatened her. He said if she called the police, he would kill Maddie," I explained.

"That was a mistake, Linds. You should have reported it," admonished Marnie.

"Maybe so, but Emily was so upset and scared, I just couldn't do it," I said apologetically.

"Okay, okay, I'll find out what I can and give you a call," said Marnie.

"Great, talk to you tomorrow," I said, then disconnected the line.

"She *is* right, you know. I really should have called the cops when we found Emily. Oh well, that's water under the bridge now. I did get a couple of pictures with my cell phone when she wasn't looking. That might help a little if we need to call the police again," I said with a shrug of my shoulders.

"Jed, we need to go back to the Harold house again," I said softly, so the kids wouldn't hear me.

"Why? We should wait for a while, since we found Emily," he said with concern.

"He keeps going back to that house, for some reason. I would like to know why he keeps doing that. Don't you think that's strange? He knows the police are in this now," I said in explanation.

"All right, but it might be dangerous," he said, trying to discourage me.

"You're right, it might be dangerous—but I want to check it out anyway. I want to look in all the places I missed," I said.

"What are you going to tell the kids? You're not taking them with you, with us, are you?" Jed asked.

"I'll tell them we're going to pick up dinner, which we will do," I said softly.

"Okay, whatever you say. You're the boss of this caper," Jed said. He tried to smile.

"Emily, Ellen, Ryan," I shouted, "Jed and I are going to pick up some food for dinner. You guys stay here, and don't let any strangers into the house. Okay?"

Three separate "okays" could be heard from different parts of the house.

I grabbed my handbag and headed for the front door.

"Come on, Jed," I said, because he seemed to be dragging his feet.

"Okay, but I think this is a bad idea," he commented under his breath.

"I'll go with or without you, Jed. So come on, if you're going with me. If not, you can babysit for two fourteen-year-old girls and an eleven-year-old boy. Is that what you want to do?"

"I could just leave," he said in a harsh whisper.

"Is that what you are going to do?" I asked angrily.

"No, I'm coming with you," he said sullenly.

Of course, it wasn't a long drive, but Jed's bad mood made it seem like forever. I tried to make small talk, but he wouldn't respond to my remarks.

"Jed, you're acting like one of my kids. What is wrong?"

"I don't know. It's just a feeling that I have. We should have stayed with the kids and let the cops do the snooping this time," he explained.

"It won't take us very long. I have a couple of flashlights we can use to peer into dark places," I said excitedly.

"You think the flashlights will protect us?" he demanded.

"No, I also have a tire iron and a crowbar. Is that helpful?" I asked.

"Yeah, I guess—so as long as he doesn't have a gun. A gun trumps a tire iron and a crowbar," he said sarcastically.

"We're here, let's hurry," I said. I opened the car door and walked around to the back. Opening the trunk, I reached for the tire iron. I left Jed the crowbar, because it was bigger and heavier. He could wield that much better than I could if it became necessary.

Jed led the way, pushing open the door and entering the room cautiously.

"I don't see anyone," he whispered.

"You go right and I'll go left. We will hurry through this. Meet me at the stairway to the second floor," I said softly.

I opened closet doors and kicked at piles of clothes on the floor, but nothing looked like it would be a reason to return to this place again. I walked to the stairway and waited for Jed.

"Did you find anything?" I asked.

"Nothing but junk. The rats have been pretty active. I found lots and lots of droppings," he said with a grimace.

"We'll check out the upstairs quickly, and then go get the food," I said, as I started up the old, worn staircase.

We didn't separate when we reached the top. We were too dumbfounded to do anything but stare.

Names were written all over the wall we were facing. I hadn't noticed that before, when we were all in the house looking for Maddie. It must be a new addition to the décor.

What startled or dumbfounded me was the fact that the names in big, bold, messy print were those of my family and friends. I mean they were *all* there, including Jed and Marnie.

There were stars next to my name, Emily's, and Jed's. We were marked for importance, I guessed.

When the ability to move returned, we searched the entire area and found nothing else. The blood was gone, as was the note. There was no sign any kind of trouble had happened. Just the list of names, shining like a beacon as the setting sun beamed through a window, highlighting the wall of names.

"Is this weird?" I whispered to Jed.

"Yes. It is. Let's get out of here," he said, trying to hurry me along.

I drove to the ready-to-go pizza place and grabbed two medium pepperoni pizzas. Then I went to a fast food drive-through and bought six cheeseburgers. It was more food than I would normally get, but we all needed some filling comfort food.

"Let's go eat, Jed. I'm starved."

Chapter 13

"That's odd," I said more to myself than to Jed.

"What?" Jed asked.

"All of the lights are turned on inside the house. The kids know better than to do that," I said, almost angrily.

"Maybe something or someone scared them. I turn on all the lights when I'm trying to figure out what is roaming around outside," said Jed.

"Help me grab the food. We need to check on the kids," I said as I picked up the pizza boxes.

I handed Jed the key to the back door, and he led the way.

"Hey, guys? What's with all of the lights?" I shouted from the kitchen.

"Mom, there was a man standing on our front porch. Emily said it was Maddie's father. He was trying to get in. He really scared me," said Ellen.

"Me, too!" chorused Emily and Ryan.

"It's okay, Ellen, we're here now. Did you see him leave?" I asked because I had seen no sign of anyone outside. Of course, I wasn't looking for anyone.

"No, I was hiding in the closet," she said, in a shaky voice.

"Get yourself some food. I bought pizzas and cheeseburgers. Eat all you want," I said to the hungry crowd standing in front of me, which included Jed.

I walked to the front of the house, where I peeked out a window. I didn't see anyone or anything, so I opened the front door to take a better look.

"Jed, that idiot threw something onto my front porch. This is the second time that man has done this," I said angrily.

It was motor oil; dirty, greasy, black motor oil was spread all over the wooden porch.

I called 9-1-1 again. What else could I do, but report the damage and harassment?

The town police pulled up in front of my house with flashing lights and sirens blaring.

I ran out the back door, which was actually located on the side of the house, and met them in the front yard. I didn't want them to step up onto the porch and get motor oil all over their shoes and then in their cars.

This time they took pictures, and I was glad because there was real proof now.

Officer Johnson wasn't in the patrol car this time. I asked the young officers to let him know this had happened, and that there was something new on the second floor of the Harold house. I told them that Maddie's father did all of this.

As soon as the officers left, I grabbed the water hose to wash the porch and get rid of the flammable fluid, which could be fired up in no time.

It was getting late, so I told the kids to get to bed.

"Leave the lights on, Mom," pleaded Emily as she kissed my cheek.

"I will, baby," I said, hugging her.

Ellen came to kiss me goodnight and whispered, "Emily was really scared, Mom."

I hugged Ellen and told her not to worry.

Ryan lunged at me for a quick hug, and raced away.

"I'm going to sleep right here in this recliner tonight. Would you like to crash on the sofa?" I asked Jed.

"Why?" he asked.

"I need to let them know that I will do whatever it takes to keep them safe," I explained.

I gathered together sheets and pillows so we could both be comfortable.

Jed dropped off to a steady snore in no time. I dozed lightly, listening for unfamiliar sounds.

I awoke to a loud banging on my front door.

I shook Jed awake so that he, too, could hear the banging.

"What is it?" sputtered Jed.

"There's someone at the door," I whispered.

"Who is it?" Jed asked.

Jed jumped up, rubbed his hands through his hair, and marched to the front door.

"Wait, look out the peephole first," I said.

Jed stepped up close to the door and squinted through the peephole.

"There's a young girl out there," he said in a whisper.

"Open it. It's probably Maddie," I said excitedly.

Jed turned the lock and removed the chain slowly. He was worried about what would happen when the door opened.

"Maddie's father might have forced her to knock on the door so he could force his way into the house," he whispered harshly.

"That's a chance we will have to take. Hurry, Jed, and open the door," I said in a loud whisper.

Standing before us was a young girl in filthy clothes that were spattered with blood. She had a cut lip and black eye that was so dark and purple that I could almost feel her pain simply by looking at her.

"Are you Maddie?" I asked.

The girl nodded her head and fell to the floor.

Chapter 14

"Help me get her up, Jed. We'll sit her down and see if she will come around so we can talk with her," I said, as I reached for her arm.

We got her to her feet and led her to the sofa where I already had spread a sheet for Jed to sleep on. I placed a pillow under her head and patted her hand to let her know I was there for her.

She opened her eyes and started to sit up.

"No, Maddie, don't sit up. Just lie there for a little while," I said softly. "Are you hungry? Are you hurt?"

She just stared at me through tear filled eyes.

I held her hand and let her cry.

I glanced at the clock and realized it was time to get the kids up for school.

"Jed, I've got to rouse the young'uns so they can get ready for school. I'm sure they won't want to go, because Maddie is here, but go they must," I said. I could say this to them in a convincing tone, I hoped.

I let Maddie go back to sleep, then walked up and down the hallway knocking on bedroom doors. I made sure to open Emily's door after I knocked to see that she was in her bed. She was there, and I breathed a sigh of relief.

"Okay guys, let's get moving," I said loudly.

Ryan was always the last person out of bed. It would take a couple more trips up and down the hall to get my eleven year old out from between the sheets.

I was hoping the girls wouldn't notice a visitor sleeping on the sofa, but that was a pipe dream.

"Mom, who is that sleeping on the sofa?" asked Ellen.

I didn't answer. I didn't have to.

"Mom, when did Maddie get here?" asked Emily.

"In the wee hours of the morning," I answered softly. "I'm going to let her sleep for a while. Then she can take a shower, and I'll let her wear some of your clothes, Emily. So—you guys need to go to school."

"But Mom," whined Emily.

"No buts, Em. Nothing is going to happen. I will call Officer Johnson and tell him Maddie is here, so they can stop looking for her."

"What if her father shows up?" asked Emily.

"I'll call 9-1-1. Now, get ready to eat breakfast. It'll only be cereal this morning. I'll make a better one tomorrow," I said apologetically.

Emily stormed into the kitchen and started making loud cereal preparation sounds including the clashing of bowls and silverware.

I always thought of Ryan as my problem child simply because was a boy. Emily seemed to be assuming that role lately. I knew I was going to have to talk to her about her temper. To tell you the truth, she came by it honestly.

The big, yellow school bus stopped in front of the house and my three grumbling children climbed aboard. I was outside standing with them as protection, I thought.

I went into the house and called my employer, telling the receptionist that I might not make it in to work. I didn't want to go into detail about why I wasn't going to be there.

"I have a sick child at home," I told Annie.

"Which one?" Annie asked.

"One of the girls is a little under the weather," I answered.

That was half way true. Maddie was a girl—just not my girl. Annie would assume the sick child was one of my daughters. I would eventually tell her the whole truth.

"I hope she feels better soon," said Annie, as she tried to end the conversation. I could hear another phone line ringing, so ending the talk was fine with me.

Jed and I drank coffee, ate cereal, and talked about what to do next.

My first task would be to call Officer Johnson.

"Officer Johnson, this is Lindsay Harris. I need to tell you that Maddie is here at my house, but her father is still a threat and he has been harassing my family," I explained in a tumble of words.

"I will stop by to talk with her, Ms. Harris," said the officer.

"Could you wait for a little while? She is asleep, and she is a mess. She needs a shower and clean clothes. Do you want me to have her clean up before you get here, or should she wait?" I asked.

"Have her wait. I need to see her, and get some photos of the damage done to her. I will be there in about an hour, if that is okay with you?" asked the officer.

"That's fine, sir."

Well, that answered that, I thought. I disconnected the line.

"Jed, I'm going to call Marnie," I said. "Maybe she has some information for me."

"It's a little early, don't you think? She probably hasn't had a chance to look anything up yet," said Jed.

"You don't know Marnie. If there is an interest sparked, she will drop everything," I said.

It took a few moments and a call transfer, but she finally answered.

"Hello?"

"Marnie, this is Linds. Did you find out anything about the Stevens family?" I asked.

"Of course! You knew I would," Marnie said with a snicker.

"Well? What is it?" I asked excitedly.

"Maddie Stevens has a *really* bad daddy. He's a pedophile, and Maddie has been the one he's abused," said Marnie.

"What can we do about him?" I asked Marnie.

"Locate him and call the cops. They will take care of the problem for you. There is a warrant out for his arrest," explained Marnie.

"What about Maddie?" I asked.

"She will be turned over to Social Services, you know that," said Marnie.

"Can't she stay with us?" I asked.

"You have to check with Social Services," said Marnie.

"How difficult do you think that would be?" I asked Marnie.

"They want good families, consisting of mother and father in most cases. In Madelyn's case, because she's so much older, I think they would let you keep her. But I don't know for sure. You would have to pass their background check," explained Marnie.

"I should be able to pass that. I *do* work for a lawyer," I said sarcastically.

"It certainly doesn't hurt, you know," agreed Marnie.

I hung up the phone and went to wake Maddie. I wanted her to be awake and alert when the police arrived. I also wanted to question her before the police had a chance to do so. I was afraid she might clam up and not tell them anything. Because I'm Emily's mother, she might open up a bit more with me. At least, that was what I hoped.

Chapter 15

"Maddie, I need you to wake up. You should eat before the police get here," I whispered as I gently shook Maddie's shoulder.

Maddie's whole body jerked as she tried to remember where she was.

"Maddie, it's okay. Don't be afraid. You are at Emily's house, and I'm Emily's mom," I said softly.

She sat up and looked at me with frightened eyes, wide and refusing to blink.

"Don't be afraid, Maddie. I'm not going to hurt you," I whispered softly.

"Who are you?" she asked in a barely audible tone.

"I'm Lindsay Harris. Emily is my daughter," I answered.

"Em's mom?" she asked.

I nodded my head in agreement.

"Thank you for letting me inside your house," she said, a little bit louder.

"We've been looking for you. Em said you needed help, so that's what we were trying to do," I said. "What can I make you to eat? How about some eggs, cereal, or soup? What do you think you can get down without a problem?"

"Eggs, I love eggs. I haven't eaten any eggs for a long time," she said. She smacked her lips to emphasize her hunger.

"Eggs it is. Scrambled or over easy? Do you want sausage or bacon? Toast?" I fired at her so she didn't have a lot of time to think about it. I was going to make what she really wanted to eat.

I proceeded to the kitchen to prepare Maddie's order of scrambled eggs, bacon, and buttered toast.

I loaded up a tray with the requested food and carried it into the living room. Maddie was sitting up and staring into the distance with glazed eyes.

"Maddie," I said softly as I tried to get her to come back to the present. "Maddie, you need to eat."

Maddie's eyes blinked and she focused on the tray of food. She started eating with both hands. She couldn't get the morsels of food into her mouth fast enough.

My eyes teared up as I watched her cram the food into her mouth.

"Slow down, Maddie. No one is going to take it away from you. If you need more, I will get it for you."

Maddie swallowed her mouthful of food and said, "Thank you, so much. It is *so* good. I would like more eggs, please."

I hurried to the kitchen to scramble another batch of eggs. I threw two more slices of bacon into a skillet for good measure. By the time I had everything cooked and served to Maddie, Officer Johnson had arrived.

"Maddie, Officer Johnson has been helping us look for you. You need to talk with him and answer all of his questions," I said, as she continued to eat.

She raised her eyes to look at Officer Johnson, who was standing in front of her looking very legal and authoritative.

"Have a seat, Officer Johnson," I said to the lawman. "I think it will be easier to talk with her if you sit on her level."

Officer Johnson backed up and sat in the chair directly across from Maddie. He asked no questions until Maddie had cleaned her plate of food for the second time.

"Young lady, tell me your name," the officer said.

"Madelyn Stevens, but everyone calls me Maddie. I like Maddie," she answered.

"Where do you live, Maddie?"

"Nowhere," she responded.

"Where did you use to live?"

"I don't remember,"

"How long have you been living on the street?" he probed.

"Forever."

"Can you read or write?" he asked.

"Of course," she answered indignantly.

"You had to have an address when you attended school. What address did you use?" he continued.

"I used the address of the place where I was staying at the time. That was the only thing I could do."

"You have no place to call home?" he pressed.

"Yes, I do, but I have a lot of different homes," Maddie said in a huff.

"Who takes care of you?" he continued.

"I do. Are you trying to find out about my father? If that is what you are doing, just come out with it," Maddie said sullenly.

"Okay, I will. Where is your father?" Officer Johnson asked.

"The last time I saw him he was out cold on the floor at the Harold house. Hopefully he died, but I'm so afraid he didn't," she said angrily.

"Why was he out cold?"

"I hit him over the head with a piece of wood I picked up at the house. He was getting ready to beat me, again, and I wasn't going to let him. Not this time, not ever again," she said with determination.

"Did you kill him?" asked the officer.

"I hope so," she said, as she fought back angry tears,

"We didn't find a body at the Harold house, but we did find some blood. Was it your blood or your father's?"

"I would guess it was from both of us," she answered. She held up her hands and arms, displaying many cuts and bruises.

"Did your father give you those bruises and cuts?" asked Officer Johnson.

"Most of them," Maddie replied sullenly.

Officer Johnson readied the camera and took many photos of Maddie from head to toe.

"I will be calling children's services so you can be looked after until we find your father," said Officer Johnson.

"She can stay with me," I said before Maddie had a chance to object to Officer Johnson's declaration.

"That's okay with me, but I will let them know when I get back to the police station. They may send me right back out here to pick her up and take her to another home," he said.

"No, please, I want to stay with Em's mom," pleaded Maddie.

"Em's mom, who is that?" Officer Johnson asked.

"I am," I said. "I want her to say here with me. I will sign whatever you need me to sign to make it happen."

"I will check on it for you, Mrs. Harris," he said sounding apologetic.

"Please do, and call me Lindsay," I said.

"Yes ma'am," he said with a fluster. "I will check back with you as soon as I find out anything at all."

"Okay," I said with a smile.

"What about you, Maddie? Should I tell your father where you are if I find him?" the officer asked.

"No! Don't do that. I know he will find me anyway. He always does. At least I might have a couple of days of freedom without him," Maddie said with such intensity that it caused all of us to look at her.

All of our eyes focused on her, which caused an explosive reaction of sobs. Maddie's body shook from her heartrending cries that filled the room.

I pulled her to me and let her cry as Officer Johnson left the room and then the house. I was sure he had no idea what to do about the flood of tears.

It was a woman thing. I just held on to Maddie until the tears subsided.

Chapter 16

"Maddie, you should go get cleaned up. The shower is down the hall, and Emily left you some of her clean clothes to wear. If things work out the way I hope they will, you will have your own clothes soon and not have to borrow Emily's or Ellen's."

While Maddie was occupied with bathing, I decided to give Marnie a call. Jed had left to go to work, and I wanted to talk to someone about what I had gotten myself into with my open invitation for Maddie to become a member of my family.

"Marnie, I have Maddie here with me. Now I need you to tell me how I can keep her here," I said excitedly when Marnie answered the insistent ring of the telephone.

"Children's services will contact you. If they don't, you need to contact them. You need to do everything legally, you know," Marnie explained. "You might want to get your boss, the illustrious Wayne Maxwell, Attorney at Law, to help you."

"Do you think I will have a problem?" I asked.

"I told you already that they like a two parent family, but Maddie is old enough to choose her parent. That should work in your favor," said Marnie.

"The paperwork worries me. Where do I find that, so I can get everything going?" I asked.

"Don't worry about that until the time comes to fill it out. How is Maddie doing? Where is her father?" sked Marnie

"To answer your first question, I think Maddie is okay. She has some cuts and bruises. It will take her a while to heal, physically and mentally. As far as her father is concerned, after she popped him on the head he disappeared. The police went looking for him, but they haven't found him. Maddie is afraid he will find her here," I explained.

"Lindsay, I think you shouldn't be spending your life solving everyone else's problems. Do you think her father will give you a problem? Where is the mother?" asked Marnie.

"I don't know anything about the mother. She doesn't appear to be in the picture anywhere. I think she may be dead, but I don't know for sure. I'll have to ask Maddie about that. Emily said Maddie told her that her mom was dead. And yes, I do think he will show up here looking for her. I'm going to be ready for him. I have my baseball bat next to the front door. I'll find something else, a crowbar maybe, to use at the back door," I said with a nervous laugh.

"So, do you want me to come stay with you to give you a hand?" asked Marnie.

"I would love that. I could really use the moral support. That will give you a chance to meet Maddie and see what you think about her situation," I said with a sigh.

"I'll be there right after work," said Marnie.

"Jed might be here, too. Is that a problem?" I asked.

"Not for me, but I don't know how Jed would feel about me being there," Marnie added.

"He's the one who told me to call you for help. I've got to go. See you later," I said.

Maddie entered the room sparkling clean and smiling.

"Feel better?" I asked

"Much," she answered contentedly.

Not having gone to work, my life was off schedule. It seemed strange to me to see a teenager walking around the house who wasn't mine when my children weren't home.

I finally got my mind to focus on the fact that my young'uns were at school, and it was my hope to be able to send Maddie there with them soon. I guessed I was overtired and brain drained as well.

"Maddie, where is your mother?" I asked, in my quest for information that might help me get my wish.

"She's dead," Maddie answered tentatively.

"How long ago did she die?" I continued.

"I was ten, so it's been four years, I guess," she whispered.

"What happened? Was she sick?" I asked.

"Yeah, in a way," she said sullenly.

"What happened?" I asked again.

"It was a drug overdose. She was sick because she was a junkie," said Maddie. The anger was beginning to manifest itself in her eyes again.

"I'm so sorry, Maddie. I'm sure you miss her a lot," I said as I tried to soothe her with words.

"No, not really, because she was always high," Maddie snapped.

"Well, if you live here with us that will not happen. Maybe I should say I hope that never happens," I said with emphasis.

"Yes ma'am, I believe you. I hope you will let me stay here," she said with pleading eyes.

"That's my plan, Maddie," I said as I hugged her.

Chapter 17

My front door burst open and my three children ran inside as if someone was chasing them.

"Slow down! What's the hurry?" I screamed at them.

"The man outside was chasing us," they said in competing voices.

"What man? Where?" I asked as I ran to the window. I leaned over as close to the window as I could possibly get so I could see a wide, panoramic expanse.

I saw no one.

"Which way did he go?" I asked. I turned my head back and forth, searching.

"I didn't notice," said Emily.

"Did you see him leave, Ellen?" I asked.

She shook her head in the negative.

"Did you see him leave, Ryan?" I asked, looking at my son.

"No, Mom, I just ran," he said excitedly.

"Okay, okay, no problem. When Jed and Marnie get here, we will look around out back," I said enthusiastically. "You guys go get out of those school clothes and I'll order a couple of pizzas. Sound good?" I asked.

I saw four heads bop up and down.

Now what do I do? I asked myself.

A knock at the door startled me out of my deep, questioning thoughts. I sprang from my seat on the sofa, where I had been awaiting the arrival of the pizza delivery boy. I opened the door without checking on who might be on the other side.

My mistake.

Suddenly I was pushed inside, an enormous handgun waving in my face.

I was startled into silence. My mouth was open, but no sounds were being emitted.

No one else was in the living room. They had all departed for their separate rooms.

I backed up as fast as my legs would allow me to move.

"What do you want?" I asked when my mouth finally began to function.

"Maddie," he snarled.

"Maddie is not here!" I shouted, as loudly as I could. I really wanted the kids, all four of them, to hear and pay attention.

"What are you doing, lady? Are you trying to warn her?" he said as he pushed the handgun closer to me.

"No, no, I was just scared. I will lower my voice," I said, holding my hands up to placate him.

"Who else is here? I saw a bunch of kids run into here. Where is Maddie?" he asked harshly.

"Maddie isn't here," I shouted again, but not quite as loudly this time.

"Pipe down, lady," he snapped.

"Okay, okay," I mumbled.

He started moving toward me again.

I backed up until I ran out of floor.

"Move on down the hall, lady," he demanded.

"Why? What are you going to do?" I whined in pure fright. I didn't want to move. I didn't want him to confront my kids. I especially didn't want him to find Maddie. I had no idea what he might do to her.

"Just walk, lady," he said as he shoved me away from the wall that I had been flattened against. "That's right, keep moving. Now, stop," he directed me.

I stood in front to Ryan's room, where I'd paused when he told me to stop. I didn't want to open the door so he could push his gun into Ryan's face.

"That's my son's room. Please don't open the door," I begged.

"Get it open now," he hissed at me.

I eased the door open. "Ryan, are you in here?" I asked in a shaky voice.

"Mom?" asked Ryan, with a frightened look on his face.

"Just do as this man says. Okay, Ryan?" I said softly.

Ryan nodded and didn't move an inch.

"Get over there, lady, and tie him up," he instructed.

I looked at him in horror.

"Why?"

"I don't want him running around here," he said angrily.

"You won't run, will you, Ryan?" I asked.

"No ma'am. I will stay right here in my room until you tell me I can leave," Ryan said. He stifled a sob.

"Tie him up!"

"What with?" I asked.

"Use your imagination, lady. Just tie him up now."

I opened a drawer and pulled out some of Ryan's long socks.

"Is this okay?" I asked. I held the socks up in shaking hands.

"Do it, lady," he hissed.

I walked over to Ryan, hugged him and said, "Lay down there, Baby. I have to do this."

Ryan was crying as hard as I had ever seen him cry.

I went to work tying the socks around his hands, behind his back. Then the man pointed to Ryan's feet. So I moved to the foot of the bed, where I tied his feet together and made sure he was as comfortable as I thought I could get away with, for the time being.

"Get it tight, lady," he snapped, and walked to the bed to tug at the ties.

"I am," I snapped back at him.

"Let's go. Move it," he said, and shoved me forward.

The next room was Ellen's. When I opened the door, the room was empty.

"Where's the kid?" he asked.

"She might be in her sister's room," I answered.

"Let's go," he said, shoving me again.

I led the way to Emily's room. I didn't want to do it, but he kept poking the gun into my ribs until I turned the doorknob.

The room was empty.

Chapter 18

"Where are they?" he screamed to me.

"I don't know," I answered. I looked around the room, just as surprised as he was.

"Is there another way out of this house?"

"The back door, but I didn't hear anyone leave. Did you?" I asked.

"You better hope they didn't leave. What are their names?" he screamed.

"Ellen and Emily."

"Ellen, Emily, get in here right now!" he shouted.

There was no sound, no response of any kind.

"I'm going to shoot your mother if you don't get in here right now," he sputtered.

I looked at him with terror-filled eyes.

"No, please. I don't know where they are," I pleaded for my life.

"Start looking for them. I'm right behind you. Find them now," he said. He jabbed me with the gun again.

I walked toward the back door. At a ninety-degree angle from the back door was the door to the basement. I'd forgotten about the basement.

"Where does that go?" he asked.

"Basement," I answered.

"Open the door," he directed me.

I opened the door slowly. I had no idea if they were down there or not.

"Ellen, Emily, are you down there?" I said loudly.

No answer.

"Where is the light switch?" he asked harshly.

"Here, right here," I said, as I snapped it on. The brightness of the light blinded me for a moment.

"Move!" he barked, pushing me forward.

I took one step down, then another. I was afraid he was going to push me down the steps to the bottom, where the floor was tile-covered concrete. I hung onto the railing all the way down, waiting for the hit. When I reached the bottom step I released a sigh. That disaster had passed; now on to another.

The basement was one large room, with the furnace installed directly in the middle.

"Move over there, and walk completely around that furnace," he said.

I did just as he directed, but they were nowhere to be found.

"Where are they?" he screamed.

"I don't know!" I screamed back at him. When my mouth closed I immediately regretted the scream. I was afraid I was going to be attacked with the butt of the gun, or that he would shoot me.

He glanced around, searching for hiding places. But there were none to be found, not in the basement.

A loud thump rattled the floor above our heads.

"Ryan must have fallen off of the bed," I mumbled, staring at the basement ceiling.

"You better hope that is what happened," he whispered. He nudged me toward the staircase to move back up to the first floor

"Walk to your son's room and check on him. Then we're going to visit your bedroom. It's the only room up here that we didn't look at," he said.

I carefully climbed the stairs and turned right to go down the hall to check on Ryan.

When I arrived at the door to his room I waited for him to make me move.

"Get in there," he hissed.

I stepped forward and looked on both sides of the bed. I did not find Ryan, however.

"Where is he?" he hissed.

"I don't know. I was with you, remember?" I said sarcastically.

"Find him," he shouted.

"How?" I sputtered.

"Check each room, including yours," he told me sternly, through clenched teeth.

The shoving started again, but this time he was more aggressive with the gun he was pushing hard against my shoulder, just above my heart.

I hurried to Emily's room; it was empty of children. On to Ellen's room, and again, it was empty. My room was the only one left that was accessed from the upstairs hallway.

My door was closed, which was normal. I was afraid to turn the doorknob and walk inside. I knew in my heart that was where they were hiding, and I didn't want to find them. I was afraid of what his next step would be, after he got all of us in the same room.

"Open it!" he shouted. He punched me in the center of my back so hard that I had to suck in a deep breath to keep from screaming out in pain.

I turned the doorknob and pushed hard against the bedroom door, causing it to bang against the wall and fly back to hit me from the front.

"That was stupid," he hissed.

"Yes, I know that," I mumbled. I slowly entered the room.

It, too, was empty of children.

The tension in the room multiplied tenfold. The movement of his gun was increasing as his patience disappeared completely.

"What is your name?" I asked, trying to break him away from the thought of shooting me right then and there.

"I'm Maddie's father, and you know that," he said angrily.

"Yes, but what is your first name, Mr. Stevens?" I said softly, trying to tone down his anger with my interest.

"Mark, my name is Mark Stevens. Now are you happy?" he asked, forcing a fake smile to his face. "Let's move. And I want you to tell me where they went," he said. "Did they go to a neighbor's house? Would they have called the police?"

"I don't know the answer to either of those questions," I said. The tears started to trickle down my cheeks.

"Go to the living room; I need to check the front of the house for any sign of the cops," Mark said.

I walked slowly, but apparently he thought I should move faster; he punched me in the back with the gun again. I was truly tired of that.

When I reached the living room, I walked to the window and looked out to see if anything was amiss. I caught a glimpse of movement on the left side, but I wasn't sure of what I had seen.

"I don't see any cops," I said, loud enough for Mark to hear.

"Move over to the side and let me look out," he said. He brushed me aside with the arm holding the gun.

"Okay, okay, if your kids got out of here, why didn't they call the cops?" he demanded.

"I don't know," I answered, with a shrug of my shoulders.

It suddenly occurred to me where they all might be. They were still in the house, but obviously out of sight.

The closet doors in every room had been standing open, so there was no reason to search inside of them—especially when I knew there were four good-sized bodies to hide.

In my bedroom, there was a door in the back of my closet that was almost hidden. You had to really be looking for it to find it; it was that well camouflaged. I'd found it merely by accident, but I didn't know my kids had found it. At least, I hoped they had found it. It was a small room, but I was sure they all could fit in there.

I wasn't sure of the reason for the room. Possibly it was a safe room for the previous owners. Whatever the reason, I was glad it was hidden as well as it was.

"You must have another hiding place in this house," he said as he looked at me.

I had the feeling that he knew what I had been thinking.

He started pecking on the walls in the living room.

"There's nothing in here. We are going to have to go into the bedrooms again."

I was getting really tired of this. I didn't want my actions to give me away.

Chapter 19

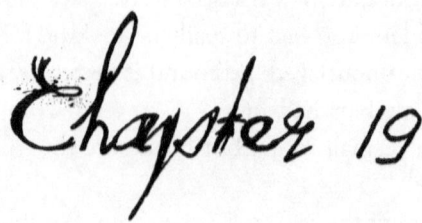

"You can get out of here and leave me alone. You can see that Maddie isn't here," I said angrily.

"I'm not going anywhere until you tell me where the kids are hiding," he replied in a vicious tone. "I will start shooting your body parts, starting with your foot, if you don't tell me where they are."

"No, please, you were with me when we searched the house. You know I couldn't find them. Please don't shoot..."

Before I could finish my plea, I heard a sound. A couple of car doors slammed; people were talking and walking toward the house.

"Who are those people? Why are they here?" he whispered harshly. "Get back from the window. I don't want them to see us."

He jerked me back, almost knocking me off of my feet.

I flailed my arms trying to fight for balance. I let out a squeal from being startled by the jerk backwards.

They were knocking at the front door. Marnie and Jed had arrived at the same time.

When the knocking didn't get a response, Jed started calling my name.

"Linds, are you in there? Your car is here, so I'm guessing you're home," he shouted.

I wanted very much to answer him, but the gun aimed at my heart stifled my scream for help.

"Lindsay, it's Marnie and Jed. Let us in," Marnie shouted

The tears of anger and fear were building up behind my eyelids.

"They better leave," he whispered.

"They will, just wait few moments. Don't try to hurt them, please," I begged. I was afraid he would let them in and then shoot them. I couldn't let that happen.

They continued to pound on the door; I cringed with every hit.

Then the pounding stopped, and their footsteps could be heard echoing down the sidewalk. My heart sank when it got quiet. I didn't want any harm to come to Jed and Marnie, but I needed help.

"They've left. Now get out of here," I said angrily.

"Not until I find Maddie. That girl tried to kill me. She needs a whipping, and I intend to give her the punishment. So you'd just better hope she shows up somewhere along the line, or you will get her whipping—or maybe even worse," he said with a haughty laugh.

Again, I caught a glimpse of movement outside my window. I hoped he hadn't seen it.

I wasn't sure what I had seen either time, but I knew there was some kind of movement out there. Maybe it was the police the first time, but it was Marnie and Jed the second. I didn't care who it was. I just needed help.

"Who is moving around out there?" he hissed. He moved closer to the window without standing directly in front of it.

"I don't know. I didn't see anyone," I lied

"Sure you did. Don't lie to me," he snarled.

"I'm not lying," I said sullenly.

"There it is again. Did you see it? It was a flash of color. It must not be a cop. Their uniforms are brown, and would be harder to see. What I saw was a light color, maybe a man's shirt. What was the man wearing, the one who knocked on your door a little while ago?" he asked.

"I don't know. You wouldn't let me answer the door," I snapped.

"You saw him. I know you saw him. What was he wearing?" he pushed.

"Some kind of jacket, that's all I remember. Marnie had on a dark jacket, as I recall. Maybe you saw one of the neighbors out there," I suggested.

"Let's go to the back door. I want to check out back for movement," he said. He pushed me in that direction with the barrel of the gun.

I wanted to walk slowly, but the gun barrel didn't let me slow down one little bit.

I stopped directly in front of the back door so he could look out the window centered in the top half.

As he leaned forward I dived over to the right, turned, and went running through the house. Of course, that was a mistake. He caught me and crashed the butt of the gun down on my head.

I was out cold. I had no idea how long I was unconscious, because I didn't wake up until I felt myself being lifted from the floor and carried to the sofa, where I was gently placed until I could finally come to my senses.

I blinked and looked around me.

Jed was pushing my hair from my face and checking out the cut on my poor aching head.

"Where is he?" I asked in a raspy, breathless voice.

"Who?" asked Jed.

"Mark Stevens. Where is he? Where are the kids?" I asked, trying to get to my feet.

"The kids are in the kitchen with Marnie, making something to eat," Jed answered.

"Is Maddie with them?" I asked.

"No, was she supposed to be?" Jed asked.

"Yes, and he will kill her if he finds her. Her father, Mark Stevens, will kill her," I said as I struggled to stand up.

"No, Linds, stay on the sofa. I'm going to take you to the emergency room as soon as the town police say we can leave. They wanted to call the EMTs, but I said not to do that because I would take you there. Okay?" he said. He gently nudged me back against the sofa.

"No, no hospital. I've got to find Maddie," I said softly. I actually wanted to scream at him to make him understand how serious the threat was to Maddie.

"Stevens isn't here, and Maddie isn't here. Just relax and let me take you to the ER," Jed said firmly.

"We'll see. What are the police doing right now?" I asked.

"They've been talking with your kids. They're trying to find out what happened," Jed explained.

"The kids don't know anything. They were hiding," I said with exasperation. "The cops need to talk with me."

As soon as I closed my mouth, there was a young policeman standing in front of me.

"Mrs. Harris, I'm Officer Smithers. I need to ask you some questions," the officer said nervously.

"Good. I'm the one you need to talk to, not my kids," I said, a little more forcefully than I should have.

"Yes ma'am. Now, can you tell me what happened?" he asked shyly.

Marnie and my kids burst into the room, full of questions.

"Okay guys, sit down and I'll tell everyone what happened until I was hit on the head," I directed them by pointing to the floor and empty chairs.

"It started with a knock—or pounding, really—on the door, and went on from there. He ushered me around at gunpoint looking for Maddie, and when he couldn't find her, he got really, really mad. So mad that he hit me over the head with his gun. Now, someone else will have to take it from here. I was out cold," I said with a sigh.

"Marnie and I will have to continue, I guess," said Jed, as he became the center of attention.

"We knew there was something wrong when Lindsay didn't answer the door. She knew we were stopping by, and her car was parked out front. We knew she was in this house, somewhere," explained Marnie.

"When no one came to the door, we walked away to our separate cars. We drove down the street a bit and parked. We climbed out and walked down a private sidewalk to the back of the house, hoping all the time that there were no six-foot fences to prevent us from walking up to Lindsay's back door," said Jed.

"We were able to almost get to Lindsay's house, but we were stopped before we could reach her yard. It seems that the cops were there watching the place. I don't know who called them, maybe one of the kids used her cell phone, but they didn't attempt to go inside because of the danger Lindsay was in," said Marnie.

"They actually interrogated us as we stood there after the frisking. I guess they were looking for weapons. We convinced them we were friends of the family. They wanted us to leave, but I absolutely refused to leave Lindsay if she was in trouble," said Jed with evident determination.

"So we waited," said Marnie.

"How did Mark Stevens get away? Where did Maddie go?" I asked. I needed them to fill in the blanks.

"He must have run out after he set up a diversion. He set a small fire in the kitchen, where you were lying on the floor, and we think he went out the front while everyone was working on the fire and pulling you out of danger," said Jed.

"So, no one saw him leave?" I asked.

"No, but we had to get in here no matter what," said Jed.

"Did you see Maddie leave?" I asked.

"No," answered Marnie.

"Did she leave with her father?" I asked.

"We don't know. We didn't see them leave, together or separately. We just don't know when or how they left," Jed explained.

"Emily, Maddie was with you, wasn't she?" I asked.

"Yes, all four of us were hiding," Emily answered.

"What happened to Maddie? Where did she go? Why did she leave?" I asked my daughter.

"She was afraid her father would be back to hurt all of us, so she left and said she wouldn't be back," said Emily.

"How did she get out of here? Didn't the police want to ask her some questions?" I asked.

"When the police were searching the house, we heard them shouting 'clear' as they checked each room. Ellen, Ryan, and I left our hiding place, while Maddie stayed inside. When things calmed down a bit, she went out a bedroom window. I don't know where she went, and I'm so worried about her," said Emily, fighting back tears.

"We'll find her, Em," I said.

Chapter 20

Over my many protests, Jed drove me to the emergency room at the local hospital, where I was pronounced alive and well with a headache. They let me leave when I refused to have a couple of stitches sewn into my cut scalp.

Marnie was with the kids, so I asked Jed to drive past the Harold house.

"Pull over and let me go inside. I want to see if Maddie is there," I said softly.

"We can do that later. I'll come back by myself," he said convincingly.

"No, we are already here. I want to check. Please Jed," I said.

I finally got him to agree, but he really didn't want to go in that house.

As soon as I opened the front door, I knew there was trouble awaiting us.

"Jed, the smell is terrible. It smells like copper," I said, as I pushed on the door.

"Yes, let me go in first. You wait here," he said. He motioned for me to stay behind.

"Not on your life, my friend," I mumbled. I walked inside the house right behind him.

It didn't take us very long to find the source of the coppery smell of spilled blood. It was the dead body of Mark Stevens.

"Oh my god," I mumbled. I stared at the body of the man who had threatened to kill me such a short time ago.

"I'll dial 9-1-1, and then I'll call your house to let Marnie know what's happening. She'll be worried if we don't tell her what's going on," said Jed.

I dreaded the arrival of the police. I was sure they were going to think I was the one causing all of these problems, which, strangely enough, might be correct. It wasn't that I wanted to start trouble. I only wanted to help a homeless teenager, a friend of my daughter's.

We lived in a small town in the rural county of Stillwell, so I knew there was a good chance that with the luck of the draw, I would be confronted by the same police officer—and I was. Officer Smithers appeared before me again with questions, many questions. So be it. There was nothing I could do about it then.

Officer Smithers decided the dead body was a topic that exceeded his pay grade, so he called the detective to take over for him.

Detective White was an older gentleman. He was very considerate with his questioning of Jed and me, until he discovered that we'd had a previous confrontation with Mark Stevens.

"Mrs. Harris, are you telling me this is the same man who held you hostage?" he asked sternly.

"Yes, sir," I replied.

"Why were you the one who found him?" Detective White asked.

"I was looking for Maddie Stevens, this man's daughter. I wanted to find her and take her home with me," I explained.

"You will need to go to the police station for further questions. You and Mr. Thompson need to make a statement explaining why you murdered Mark Stevens," said Detective White.

"Me murder Mark Stevens? No! I didn't, and neither did Jed. We found him that way. I swear to God he was dead when we got here," I sputtered as I tried to take in what he was saying.

"We will talk about all of that the station. I'll let the forensic people finish up here and I want the two of you to come with me," said Detective White.

I looked at Jed and shrugged.

Why did I have to look for Maddie tonight? I asked myself.

I knew the answer to that question. I was worried about Maddie. That was all there was to it.

A new worry crossed my mind. *Did Maddie kill her father?*

Chapter 21

The trip to the police station was strange, because Jed and I were locked up in the back seat of the police car like we were common criminals.

"Jed, as soon as we get to the station I'll give my boss, Wayne, a call. He's a lawyer, a good lawyer, and he can tell us what is what, if you know what I mean," I whispered.

"We don't need a lawyer, do we?" asked Jed.

"Maybe. Detective White thinks I killed Mark Stevens, and because you're with me, you are involved," I explained in a whisper.

"But all we did was find him," he sputtered.

"Yeah, I know."

We were escorted from the police car without handcuffs. That would have been so embarrassing, if we had been cuffed.

We were led to an interrogation room, where I was told to take a seat. Jed was taken to an adjoining room. For some reason, they felt it necessary to separate us. I guessed it was because they wanted to compare our stories.

"Mrs. Harris, do you know how Mark Stevens was killed?" asked Detective White.

"No, I don't. I want to call a lawyer," I said stubbornly.

"Why would you want to do that?" asked the surprised detective.

"Because he is my boss, and he would know how and if I should answer these questions," I said sullenly.

"Who is your boss, the lawyer, I mean?" asked Detective White.

"Wayne Maxwell," I answered.

"I'll give him a call for you," said the detective as he rose to leave the room.

I sat in that interrogation room alone for several minutes before the detective returned.

"Mrs. Harris, you and Mr. Thompson can leave, but we will be in touch with you," said Detective White with a broad smile.

"Why?" I sputtered.

"We have arrested the perpetrator," he answered.

"Who would that be?" I asked.

"His daughter," he answered.

"Tell her I'll call a lawyer," I said angrily.

"Why would you do that?" asked the detective,

"She will need the help," I answered.

Jed and I left the police station after we were denied the opportunity to speak with Maddie.

My next step was to call Wayne Maxwell.

"Lindsay, what is the problem?" Wayne asked in a gruff tone, as soon as he discovered it was me calling.

"There is a young lady by the name of Maddie Stevens who will be charged with killing her father. She will need a good lawyer, and I can't think of anyone better than you," I said as I laid on the praise,

"How old is this young lady?" asked Wayne.

"Fourteen," I answered softly.

"I would have to be retained by her parents. Where can I find them?" he probed.

"Her mother died of an overdose several years ago. Her father, Mark Stevens, was killed today at the unoccupied Harold house," I explained.

"How did you get involved with this young lady, Lindsay?" he asked curtly.

"She's a friend of Emily's. I promised Emily I would help this girl any way I could."

"Who is going to pay?" asked Wayne, getting down to the only reason he was a lawyer.

"I will, if I have to," I snapped.

"Did she kill her father?" he asked angrily.

"I don't know but I wouldn't blame her if she did," I sputtered. Asking nicely wasn't going to work. I had to use the truth. "Can you go to the police station and talk with her? They wouldn't let me in to see her."

"Are you planning to work tomorrow, Lindsay?" he asked sarcastically.

"Yes, sir," I said softly.

"All right. I will go see this Maddie Stevens," he said sternly.

"Thanks, Wayne. I will see you tomorrow," I said as our conversation came to an end.

I worked for and with Wayne Maxwell, but truthfully, I didn't like him very much. He didn't seem to treat his employees like they were people. He wanted us to be machines who turned out piles and piles of paperwork. If we had a personal problem, he considered it a firing offense and your job could be in jeopardy. I had balanced precariously on the edge of unemployment on a couple of occasions.

I hoped he would not treat Maddie like he did us minions. She had enough problems without having to deal with Wayne treating her as badly as he treated his employees. Wayne always treated his clients like royalty, so I was hoping he would do that for Maddie.

My mind wandered back to my family and friends.

Jed and Marnie were the friends I depended on when a crisis managed to enter my life.

Jed was the one with the manly strength to help guide me to the right, reasonable decisions.

Marnie was my confidant, the one to whom I could voice my major, all-consuming worries, and she would be sympathetic if need be. She would also tell me how stupid I was, if she thought I was mishandling a situation.

I don't know what I would have done the last couple of years without either of them. I wanted to make sure I didn't damage or destroy the relationships I had cultivated with both of them.

My kids, Emily, Ellen, and Ryan, were a blessing most of the time. I believed all parents felt that way, if they were honest.

Emily was the serious one; Ellen was happy-go-lucky, and Ryan was all boy. Even though Emily and Ellen were identical in appearance, they were not identical in emotional matters.

Because of Emily's serious look at life, I had to deal with her problems without her asking me to do so many times.

My hope above all hopes was that Ellen would continue along the path to happiness so I could deal with Emily's problems.

Ryan would jump into the problem pool once in a while, but his actions hadn't quite moved past boy to teenager. I guessed that I was still lucky on that account.

Jed and Marnie departed for separate abodes and I ushered my children to their rooms, to be followed by nighttime preparations and sleep.

Sleep—that sounded good.

Chapter 23

The morning arrived on wings because the hours seemed to fly by without hesitation.

"Okay, time to rise and shine," I shouted, as I stood in the hallway.

Three separate 'okays' could be heard mumbled by each one of my children.

Breakfast was cold cereal and toast, because it seemed everyone was moving slower than usual. Too much excitement in the last few days had colored our lives, causing the slowness.

"Mom, what about Maddie?" asked Emily.

"She is in custody, and I have asked Wayne to handle her case," I told Emily. At that point, that was all I could tell her. "I'll try to find out more today."

The school bus was looming at the end of the road, so I rushed the three of them out the door.

I immediately jumped into my car and headed for work as Wayne Maxwell's legal secretary and assistant. Anna, the receptionist, was already there and she plastered a smile across her face as soon as she saw me enter the office, despite the fact that I had a tendency to call her Annie . I was sure she didn't want to spend another full day there with Wayne without me as a buffer.

I went to my office to see what was waiting for me. I knew there would be a lot to do. Wayne had no problem with delegating.

I heard the front office door burst open, and Wayne's loud voice boomed down the hallway. "Lindsay Harris, are you here?"

"Right here, Wayne. You had to see my car parked right out front," I shouted, in answer to his bellow.

He did not continue to walk to his office. He found it necessary to enter my small room and plant himself in the chair in front of my desk.

"Lindsay, how did you get involved with this mess?" he asked.

"Through Emily, like I told you yesterday. She's Emily's friend from school," I explained again.

"This little girl is in a mess of trouble. She says she didn't kill him, *this time*, even though she had tried to kill him previously. It seems that her father doesn't make friends easily, but he does accumulate enemies galore. If she didn't kill him, it would be hard to prove who actually did," he said with a sigh.

"Did Maddie see who did it?" I asked.

"She said he saw another homeless man running away when she arrived at the Harold house. I don't think I can put a lot of stock into that statement. She had blood all over her hands and clothes from trying to help him, she said. But again, I'm not sure about that story at all," Wayne said.

"Why don't you believe her, Wayne?" I asked.

"It's her attitude. She has been living on the streets on her own for quite a while. She will tell you whatever you need to hear so she can survive," he said.

"Can I get in to see her?" I asked.

"Yes, I left your name so you can go talk with her. She was asking for you anyway," he replied.

"Did she tell you what the homeless guy looked like?" I asked.

"Yes, but it was a very vague description. Makes me think there wasn't one," he answered.

"What is going to happen to her now?" I asked.

"They will keep her in jail as an adult. They can't let her go, because they're charging her with murder," he answered.

"I'll go see her on my lunch hour. She might need me to pick up some girl essentials," I said.

Chapter 24

I arrived at the jail and was searched thoroughly before I was allowed to talk with Maddie. The officers knew me because I worked for Wayne, so they brought Maddie into a room without any restraints. I was so glad to see that happen.

Maddie immediately threw her arms around me and burst into tears.

"I didn't kill him, Lindsay. I swear I didn't kill him. Not this time," she said between tearful intakes of breath.

"The homeless man you saw leaving, what did he look like?" I asked, when the sobs had subsided a bit.

"A dirty, scummy, nasty man," Maddie replied.

"I need more than that if I'm going to find him," I told her softly,

"Do you believe me?" she asked, with wonder in her expression.

"Of course I do. If you can give me more information about him, we—Jed, Marnie, Emily, Ellen, Ryan, and I—will find him," I said with encouragement.

"Why would you do that?" asked Maddie.

"You are a friend of Emily's. Now, you are *my* friend, too. We will all band together and help each other, including you," I explained.

"He isn't very old—the homeless man, I mean—maybe in his twenties. He has long, scraggly, dirty hair, and his eyes were bright blue. He had them wide open with fright, when I saw him. He had on old torn blue jeans and a couple of shirts, one over another. It looked like the shirt was once a medium blue color, but it was so dirty. He wasn't very tall, maybe 5'7" or 8". That's about all I can remember," she said sadly.

"I believe I saw him running away from there. That should be enough description. We will find him. Why didn't you give this description to Wayne when he was talking with you?" I asked.

"I could tell he didn't believe me. My thought about it was why bother?" she said with a shrug,

"I can understand that feeling. Now, back to the homeless man. I have one more question. Had you seen him before the killing?" I asked.

"Yes, he was in the Harold house before when I stayed there. He was on the second floor; I stayed downstairs. He never gave *me* a problem, but he didn't seem to want my father around. I'm guessing it was because he'd heard the beatings and cussings I had received a couple of times. They acted like two animals circling each other over a kill, and the house was the kill. At least, that's what it seemed like to me," Maddie said.

"Territorial problems, some people just can't share. Maybe he was even trying to help you in his own strange way. Right?" I said as I shook my head. "He didn't try to chase you away, did he?"

"No, never," she replied.

I said goodbye and went back to work to find my way to the bottom of the pile of papers on my desk. As I returned to the office, Annie took off for lunch and promised to bring me back a sandwich. I was so hungry, but I couldn't waste time waiting for food to be served because I was already running late.

"Annie, Jed, Marnie, and I will be searching for the homeless man tonight. Do you want to come along?" I asked as a friendly gesture.

"Yes," Annie replied, with no hesitation. "What time should I be at your house?"

"Around six," I said. I continued my work with my head down.

Chapter 25

"Okay," I said loudly, "the kids want to help, so I need an adult with each child. Emily, you go with Marnie; Ellen, you and Annie are partners; Jed and Ryan are together, and I will be the backup for everyone," I said expecting an argument. When no arguments arose, we all piled into three cars and took off for the Harold house.

Everyone was acting like we were going to a party, not looking for a murderer. I knew that attitude had to be tempered, but not so much as to frighten them. This definitely was not party time.

When we arrived at the Harold house, I motioned for them all to circle up around me so we could talk.

"This is not a happy event, guys. We are looking for a killer to help clear a friend of a murder charge. Each and every one of you must pay close attention to your surroundings," I said sternly.

That statement calmed the levity a bit, and every set of eyes started glancing from side to side. I hoped I had made them think a bit, and understand that there might be danger waiting inside the old, dilapidated Harold house.

Marnie and Emily entered first and turned to the right; Ellen and Annie followed and veered to the left; the rest of us headed upstairs to the second floor, with Jed and Ryan leading the way. My gut told me the second floor was where trouble, in the form of the homeless man, would be found.

"You need to move a little slower," I cautioned Jed and Ryan. "He's probably hiding up here."

They both looked at me with a frown. I guessed they had thought the very same thing.

I could hear female voices on the first floor, shouting "clear" like they had heard on all of the police programs on television.

Jed stopped in front of the wall that listed our names. Mark Stevens had performed that bit of vandalism.

"Mom," whispered Ryan, "why are our names written on the wall?"

I guess he didn't have any paper and he didn't want to forget who we were," I said. I really had no idea why he did it. That explanation sounded as good as any other one I might come up with.

We proceeded slowly. I think Ryan had realized that there might be danger ahead. I knew Jed felt that way, too.

Jed was leading; I was bringing up the rear, and Ryan was safely tucked in the middle.

The house was dark, with very few windows to allow the light inside.

We peeked into the first room. It appeared to be filled with junk in the form of paper and plastic.

The next room contained a bed of sorts. There was a battered, old mattress and a few pieces of cloth, apparently used for blankets, piled in a corner.

The next room was the last one on the second floor. I was a little bit hesitant to enter it, because I really knew in my heart that he was in there. He would be ready to spring at us and attack us. I hoped the fact that there were three of us would stop him from trying to do us harm.

"Wait a second," I whispered as we drew near the door to the third room.

They both stopped walking immediately. That led me to believe they were just as frightened as I was.

"Listen," I said softly.

I could hear movement in the room. I couldn't tell who or what was causing the sound, but I was about as alert to any type of sound as I could be.

Jed lowered his head and stepped into the room, which was totally dark. No light was entering through a window, if there was a window.

Suddenly he moved forward, but not under his own power. Ryan also moved forward, falling, and I fell over Ryan.

I had no idea what had just happened to cause Jed to move forward. Ryan and I scrambled to get to our feet, but we were pushed back down by someone.

"Hey, let me up," I shouted angrily.

I could hear footsteps racing up the stairs to help us.

"Get out of my house," growled the person who wouldn't allow me to rise from the floor.

"What did you do to Jed?" I screamed.

"He's sleeping. You will be sleeping if you all don't leave," he hissed.

"I can't leave if you won't let me up," I said angrily.

He moved his weight from my back and said, "Get out of here now."

I stood up, trying to look around to see where Jed and Ryan were.

"Where are my son and my friend?" I demanded.

"Sleeping," he answered. He pushed me toward the hallway that would take me to the staircase.

I crashed into the group coming to help.

"Wait, don't go any further. He has Jed and Ryan," I said loudly.

The four ladies halted their forward momentum and stared at me.

"What?" asked Marnie.

"The room at the end—we were going to look in there, and someone pulled Jed and Ryan inside. He told me to leave, and when I asked about Jed and Ryan, he said they were sleeping. All I could figure was that he knocked both of them unconscious," I answered.

I dialed 9-1-1 for help.

"Officer Johnson or Smithers, please. This is an emergency. I need to speak with Officer Johnson or Smithers, or Detective White," I said when the detective's name popped into my head.

"White here," said a gruff voice.

"Detective White, this is Lindsay Harris. I'm the friend of Maddie Stevens. We need some help at the Harold house. There is a man here holding my friend, Jed, and my son, Ryan, in a room and he won't let them leave," I explained hurriedly. "He actually said they were sleeping, so I think he's knocked them out with something."

"What are you doing at the Harold house?" he asked gruffly.

"Looking for the homeless man that Maddie saw. We found him, but I need your help getting Jed and Ryan away from him," I answered.

"I'm on my way," he said in a tone that made me think he was irritated by having to help me.

"Go back downstairs, everybody. We need to wait for the police to get here," I said, pointing to the staircase.

"We've got to help them," said Annie.

"I know, that's why I called the police," I said.

"How long will it take them to get here?" Annie asked.

"I don't know," I answered softly.

"Let's go get them out of there," said Emily, who was angry enough to whip the world.

"That might be a good idea," I said thoughtfully. "I don't think he likes men, and he might try to kill both of them just like he killed Mark Stevens. I don't think he considered me a threat. That's why he let me leave."

"Good. He shouldn't be afraid of any of us because we're females," said Marnie.

"Maybe not," I whispered. "Let's go find out."

The railing was loose on the staircase, so I grabbed one of the posts to use as a weapon if I needed one. The other ladies followed suit, and we were suddenly all armed with a weapon of sorts.

When we reached the doorway to the room I shouted, "Jed, Ryan, are you okay?"

All I heard in response was a moan.

I started to move forward when a dark figure blocked my progress.

"Get out of the way!" I shouted. I started swinging my makeshift weapon.

Right behind me were four more swinging weapons, causing the dark figure to back up to stand clear of the swings.

"Go away!" said a raspy voice.

"Not without Jed and Ryan," I said over his shouts.

All five of us moved forward, swinging our weapons hoping to feel the contact of wood against flesh and bone.

My foot hit against something.

"Jed is that you?" I asked, as I continued to swing the post.

A grunt was the only response I heard.

"Don't let that creep leave the room," I said in a harsh whisper. "Jed is under my feet and I think Ryan is there, too. You guys back that creep up into a corner, and keep him there until the police get here."

I took the small flashlight that was attached to my keyring, which I always kept in my pocket, and shined it onto what I had kicked. It was Ryan; he was the one who was moaning. I kneeled down to help him, first removing the dirty cloth gag from his mouth. He was tied up with tape. It looked like colored duct tape.

I pulled at the tape to free his hands. When his hands were free, he started working on his feet.

I moved the beam of the flashlight around as I looked for Jed.

I found him in the corner, directly opposite of where the girls had the creep pinned,

Jed was also gagged, but there was duct tape across his mouth. I gave the tape a quick jerk and he winced from pain.

I started to untie his hands, which were also duct taped.

A commotion in the opposite corner drew my attention. The creep was trying to escape from his temporary prison.

"Stop him! Don't let him get through there!" shouted Annie.

"Get back! Move it, creep!" shouted Marnie. She swatted at the man and made a connection with the wooden stick, impacting flesh and bone.

"Ow-w-w-w!" the homeless man screamed, clutching his arm.

A flurry of booted footsteps could be heard coming toward us. When I spotted the noise makers, I saw protruding guns pointed at all of us.

"Lindsay Harris, where are you?" shouted the gruff voice of Detective White.

"Right here!" I shouted back. "He's trying to escape. Stop him, please!"

The darkness was preventing me from seeing all of the action but, the male grunts and growled commands led me to believe they soon had the homeless man in handcuffs.

"Mrs. Harris, you should have waited for us to get here," he said as a reprimand.

"I couldn't. I was afraid he would kill Jed and Ryan. I really think he would have if he had the chance," I said in a rush of words.

"I need you all to come to the police station and make a statement. All of you need to come, kids included," he said sternly.

"We will meet you there, Detective White," I said.

I watched the officers wrestle the homeless man into the back of the police car.

We all piled into the three cars, and I led the caravan of vehicles to the police station.

"When will you release Maddie Stevens?" I asked after we had all signed sworn affidavits.

"As soon as we interrogate the man we arrested, I will call you and tell you what the next step will be," said Detective White.

I loaded my children into my car along with Annie, because we had left her car parked in my driveway.

Jed went home, as did Marnie, with shouts of "Call me tomorrow," hurled in my direction.

Annie climbed out of my car and directly into her vehicle so she could go home. It was getting late, and my children had to go to bed so they would be ready to face a new school day. Of course, I had to get some sleep as well, so I could be bright and awake to face Wayne Maxwell, Attorney at Law.

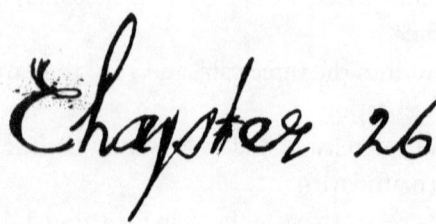

Chapter 26

Everyone was up and ready to go early. The kids had stories to tell, and they would do so at every opportunity.

I needed to let Wayne know what was going on with his client, Maddie Stevens, so he could hurry along the release process.

Annie would surely want to talk to me about the events and what would come next.

I just wanted my life to get back to normal for a while, so I could take the necessary steps to get Maddie a home: my home, if possible.

"Lindsay, Marnie is on line one," Annie said over the intercom, almost in a whisper. She didn't want Wayne to hear what she was saying, because she thought it might be a personal call.

"Thanks," I replied.

I reached for the telephone receiver and uttered a cheerful "Hello," to Marnie.

"Lindsay, I've done some digging into Maddie's background. I found an aunt who lives in West Virginia," said Marnie.

"Oh, really?"

"Aren't you glad that I've found her family?" asked Marnie.

"Yes, but what if she doesn't want Maddie?" I asked.

"We have to check with her first, you know. She *is* a member of Maddie's family," said Marnie.

"I know, but she's been through so much. I would like her to stay with my family, if possible," I said solemnly.

"Family is better, you know that," said Marnie.

"Not always," I mumbled. I had visions of Maddie's father racing through my mind.

"I'm going to give Maddie's aunt a call. In the meantime, if you get a chance to talk with Maddie, ask her about what she thinks of her aunt," said Marnie.

"Okay, I'll probably see her sometime today. I'm hoping they'll release her into my custody," I said.

"Don't get your hopes up. You know family comes first in custody decisions," said Marnie.

"Yes, I know," I answered.

When the conversation with Marnie ended, I received another phone call almost immediately. This time it was Jed.

"Linds, what's happening?" he asked cheerfully.

"Just working. What's going on with you?" I asked.

"Has Maddie been released yet?" he asked.

"No," I answered.

"When will she get out of jail?" he probed.

"Later today, I hope," I said.

"What then?" he asked.

"What do you want to know, Jed?"

"Are you going to get to keep her?" he asked.

"Marnie has located an aunt in West Virginia. Maddie will probably have to go live with her," I answered.

"I'm so sorry, Linds. I know you wanted her to stay with you," he said, as he tried to console me with words.

Maddie was released into the custody of her aunt, but she stopped at the house to say goodbye to me after I arrived home from work.

Emily and Maddie vowed to stay in touch, and tears rolled down my cheeks as I saw Maddie and her aunt drive away from my life. I hoped they wouldn't be gone forever, but only time would tell.

My thoughts traveled back to the mystery of Maddie and all of the snooping we had to do to uncover the answers to helping her survive.

It was truly wonderful to discover that *snooping can be helpful—sometimes.*

ABOUT THE AUTHOR

Linda Hudson Hoagland of Tazewell, Virginia, a graduate of Southwest Virginia Community College, has won acclaim for many her of novels: *Onward & Upward, Missing Sammy, Snooping Can Be Doggone Deadly, Snooping Can be Devious, Snooping Can Be Contagious, Snooping Can Be Dangerous, The Best Darn Secret, An Awfully Lonely Place, The Backwards House, Death by Computer, Checking on the House*, and *Crooked Road Stalker*. She has also written biographies, stage plays, and has had her short stories, essays, and poems published in anthologies including *Cup of Comfort, Christmas Blooms, Broken Petals* and *Sproutlings: A Compendium of Little Fictions* (an Australian publication). Her other books include *Watch Out for Eddy, Just a Country Boy: Don Dunford–Updated 2014, Living Life for Others, Quilted Memories, 90 Years and Still Going Strong*, a selection of short writings entitled *A Collection of Winners*, and a poetry collection *I Am...Linda Ellen*.

Hoagland is a retired Tazewell County School Board Purchase Order Clerk where she worked for almost 23 years.

She has two sons, Mike and Matt who are married to Sherry and Becky.

AWARDS

2016 – Northern Stars Poetry Contest
Honorable Mention – *The Deer*

2015 – West Virginia Writers
Pearl S. Buck Award – *Killing Creatures*

2015 – Alabama Writers Conclave
Honorable Mention – *Night of the Fools*

2015 – Tennessee Mountain Writers
Honorable Mention – *Mom's Know*

2015 – The Storyteller Magazine
First Place – *Dad's Garden*

2015 – Green River Writers
Third Place – *Nancy's Reality*

2014 – Writer's Digest Popular Fiction Awards
Honorable Mention – *Just for G.P.*

2014 – The Writers' Workshop
Honorable Mention – Starting Over – *Again*

2014 – Page Crafters Award
Second Place – *His Read Headed Wife*

2014 – Sherwood Anderson
Short Story Contest – *The Noise*

2014 – Alabama Writers' Conclave
Third Place – *Pick It Up, Please!*

2014 – Alabama Writers' Conclave
Fourth Place – *November 4th*

2013 – *The Storyteller Magazine* – People's Choice Award for Poetry
Third Place – *Politicians*

2013 – Chautauqua Creative Writing Contest
Honorable Mention – Adult Essay

2012 – Dream Quest One
First Writing Prize – *I Am Mom*

2012 – Virginia Writers Club
Second Place – *No Service*

2012 – Westmoreland Arts & Heritage Festival
Honorable Mention – *Welcome to Whistler*

2012 – Tennessee Mountain Writers
Second Place – *And the Next Day...*

2012 – The Seacoast Writers Association
Third Place – *Getting Myself Primed*

2012 – West Virginia Writers
Honorable Mention – *I'm Not Ready*

2011 – Women's Memoirs – All Things Labor
Honorable Mention – *Penance*

2011 – Alabama Writers Conclave
Honorable Mention – First Chapter of a Novel – *Writing the Circuit*

2011 – Alabama Writers Conclave
Juvenile Fiction – *The Lady in the Sun*

2011 – Appalachian Heritage Writers Symposium
Second Place – Adult Essay – *Surprise Package*

2011 – Writers-Editors Network International Writing Competition
Honorable Mention – Nonfiction – *Getting Myself Primed*

2011 – Tennessee Mountain Writers
Writing for Young People – *I Dare You*

2010 – The Jesse Stuart Prize for Young Adult Writing
Second Place – *How's That For Real*

2010 – Tampa Writers Alliance – Novel
Honorable Mention – *Quilt Pieces*

2010 – Alabama Writers Conclave – Nonfiction
Third Prize – *Four Large Eggs*

2008 – Nominee Governor's Award for the Arts

2007 – Sherwood Anderson Short Story Contest
First Place – Category V

Many other awards have not been listed.

SNOOPING CAN BE UNCOMFORTABLE

Lindsay, as a legal secretary/assistant, gets pulled into an ugly, fatal divorce that involves Ellen, her 14-year-old daughter's best friend.